CW00942622

liff

By the same author

Free Love
Like
Other stories and other stories
Hotel World
The whole story and other stories
The accidental
Girl meets boy
The first person and other stories
There but for the
Artful
Shire
How to be both
Public library and other stories
Autumn
Winter
Spring
Summer
Companion piece

ali smith

Gliff

HAMISH HAMILTON
an imprint of
PENGUIN BOOKS

HAMISH HAMILTON

UK | USA | Canada | Ireland | Australia
India | New Zealand | South Africa

Hamish Hamilton is part of the Penguin Random House group of companies whose addresses can be found at global.penguinrandomhouse.com.

First published 2024
001

A short piece of this text was first published as the story 'Art Hotel', in *A Cage Went in Search of a Bird: Ten Kafkaesque Stories* (Abacus, 2024), with grateful thanks to Anna Kelly and Abacus

Set in 13/16pt Sabon MT Pro
Typeset by Jouve (UK), Milton Keynes
Printed and bound in Great Britain by Clays Ltd, Elcograf S.p.A.

The authorized representative in the EEA is Penguin Random House Ireland, Morrison Chambers, 32 Nassau Street, Dublin D02 YH68

A CIP catalogue record for this book is available from the British Library

HARDBACK ISBN: 978–0–241–66557–2
TRADE PAPERBACK ISBN: 978–0–241–66558–9

Penguin Random House is committed to a sustainable future for our business, our readers and our planet. This book is made from Forest Stewardship Council® certified paper.

For Luigi, Luis and Alex Sacco
and the story at the heart
of every chance encounter,

to keep in mind
Bette MacDonald,
horse woman,

for everyone at the
Portobello Bookshop
– long story short,

and for Sarah Wood,
brave art.

The history of mankind is the instant between
two strides taken by a traveller.
Franz Kafka, trans. Ernst Kaiser / Eithne Wilkins

Because – how do you explain that it is never inspiration that drives you to tell a story, but rather a combination of anger and clarity?
Valeria Luiselli

Words and rocks contain a language that follows a syntax of splits and ruptures. Look at any word long enough and you will see it open up into a series of faults, into a terrain of particles each containing its own void . . . The shapes of the chasms themselves become 'verbal roots' that spell out the difference between darkness and light.
Robert Smithson

Which house is burning? The country where you live, or Europe, or the whole world? Perhaps the houses, the cities have already burned down – who knows how long ago? – in a single immense blaze that we pretended not to see. Some are reduced to just bits of frame, a frescoed wall, a roof beam, names, so many names, already eaten by the flames. And yet we cover them so carefully with white plaster and false words that they seem intact. We live in houses, in cities burned to the ground, as if they were still standing; the people pretend to live there and go out into the streets masked amid the ruins as if these were the familiar neighbourhoods of times past. And now the form and nature of the flame has changed; it has become digital, invisible and cold – but exactly for this reason closer still; it encircles and envelops us at every moment.
Giorgio Agamben, trans. Kevin Attell

Now haud ye cheerie, neebors a'
And gliff life's girnin' worriecraw.
Shelley's *Flowers by the Wayside*, 1868

horse

Our mother came down to the docking gate to say cheerio to us. For a moment I didn't recognize her. I thought she was just a woman working at the hotel. She had her hair scraped back off her face and tied in a ponytail and she was wearing clothes so unlike her and so not quite right for her shape that it took me that moment to work out they were her sister's work clothes, the uniform they made the women and girls here wear, white shirt, long black pinafore apron/ skirt thing. The men and boys who worked here got to look more casual. Their uniform was designer jeans and white T-shirts made of stuff that was better than what ordinary T-shirts get made of. The women and girls weren't allowed make up or earrings or necklaces. Our mother looked smaller, duller, scrubbed clean and cloistery, like serving women from humbled countries look in films on TV.

How is she doing today? Leif asked.

How long will she be ill? my own sister asked.

Our mother gave my sister a look for being rude.

Two weeks, Leif said, three? As long as till September?

The far away word September hung in the air round us in the weird tradespeople space. My sister looked at her feet. Leif looked at the walls, concrete and stone, the huge lit candles in the glass jars burning pointless against the daylight.

Christ, he said.

He said it like a question.

Our mother shook her head, nodded her head, nodded from one to the other of the two statues the hotel had on either side of the docking entrance, shook her head again then put her finger to her mouth as if to smooth the place beneath her nose, graceful, but really to quieten Leif and us.

They were life size, the statues, substantial white stone, shining. They looked churchy. They looked related but they were separate. One was of a sad looking beautiful woman with a cloth round her head exactly like a Virgin Mary with her arms cupped, open and empty, one hand upturned and her eyes downturned, closed or gazing down at her own empty lap, at nothing but the folds in her clothes. The other was of the bent body of a man. He was obviously meant to be dead, his head turned to one side, his arms and legs meant to look limp. But the angle he was at on the floor made him look stiff and awkward, sprawled but frozen.

Leif gave him a push and he rocked from side to side. Our mother looked panicked.

Rigor mortis, Leif said. So nowadays this is what passes for pity. And this is what happens to art when you think you can make a hotel of it.

Our mother told Leif in a formal sounding voice, as if she didn't know us, that she'd be in touch. She did a thing with her head to remind us about the cameras in the corners, she kissed us with her eyes, and then, like we were guests who'd been quite nice to her, she hugged each of us separately, polite, goodbye.

We traced our way back through the crowds of tourists to where we'd left the campervan by using a Google streetmap. It was easier to navigate by the shops than by the streets so we went towards Chanel instead, biggest thing on the map. Now Gucci. Now Nike. Strange when we finally found the far side where Alana's flat was, a place not even registering on Google as a place, that Leif got in on the driving side, because it was our mother who always drove. She was good at the campervan which was notoriously tricky. He was going to be less good, less sure of it, which is maybe why he made us both sit in the back even though the passenger seat was empty. Maybe this was to stop us fighting over who got to sit up front. Maybe he just didn't want to have us watching him too close while he was concentrating.

He turned the ignition. It started.

We'll give it a month then we'll come back and collect her, whether Alana's job's still on the line or not, he said as we left the city.

But it was a good thing. It was all in a good cause. Alana was our mother's sister. We had only met her once before, back when we were too small to know, and she'd been too ill for us to see much of her this time. But because of our mother she'd keep her job, and we could have our mother all the other summers, we could learn from this summer that this was what family did and what you did for family, and it was a very busy place Alana worked. It needed its staff. We'd seen that when we'd walked past the night before trying to catch a glimpse of our mother working and hoping to wave hello as we passed.

We couldn't spot her, there were so many people, the inside restaurant full, the outside front courtyard restaurant full too, of people the like of which I had never seen, not in real life. They were so beautiful, coiffed and perfect, the people eating in the restaurant of the place our mother was working. They were smoothed as if airbrushed, as if you really could digitally alter real people.

I saw a table with what looked like a family at it, a woman, the mother presumably, elegant, raising her fork, it had a piece of something on it and she put it to her mouth rather than in her mouth, as if she were automatonic, then her arm and hand put it back down on the plate, then raised it again. Next to her, a boy, elegant, stirring indifferently at what was on his plate and staring into space. Then the man, the father maybe, rotund but elegant, dressed as if at an awards ceremony off TV and scrolling a phone instead of eating. Then a girl, I couldn't see what she was doing but she was elegant even though she had her back to me.

It was like they all had their backs to me, even the ones facing me.

Their disconnect was what elegant meant.

Like something vital had been withdrawn from them, for its own protection maybe? maybe surgically, the withdrawal of the too-much-life from people who could afford it by people masked and smelling of cleanness inserting the cannula in a clinic, its reassuring medical smell, one after the other the perfect family offering an arm.

But then where did it go? What did the surgeon do with the carefully removed life-serum? How could you protect it, wherever you stored it, from everything? the disastrous heat, the gutter dirt, the pollution, the things that changed, the terrible leavetakings, the journeying?

They were so still, so stilled. Was that what endurance was?

Is it still life? I'd said out loud as we passed.

Is what? Leif said.

I'd nodded towards the restaurant we'd never have got into.

Even though they're breathing and moving they're like the things in one of those old paintings of globes and skulls and fruits and lutes, I said.

Leif laughed then and winked down at me.

Art hotel, he said.

Usually when we were this near home our mother would be driving and Leif would be saying the thing he always said on this stretch of the road, about how when you go to a different country the houses people live in all look like houses out of folk tales and then when you get home again you wonder if people have ever looked at where you live yourself and seen it as a place in a story.

Our mother would be getting at Leif about always saying the same thing at the exact same point on the journey.

It wasn't that they were fighting, it wasn't serious, it would be warmth coming from them in the front of the van, Leif saying, no, because when you went to a new place it was like things were new to the eye and when you got back home your eyes stayed new for a while but not for long enough, they soon got old again.

Today though Leif wasn't saying anything.

But the place on the road where this always happened was so near home that it wouldn't feel like home without somebody saying it. So I said to my sister, hoping Leif would hear me, wasn't it interesting that different places you went to could make things be like they were out of a story.

But he didn't hear, or if he did he didn't say, and anyway my sister was asleep leaning against me on the seat.

I loved the campervan. We both did. We loved the way the back window was a square of glass that opened. We loved the tables, how they folded away for safety when we were driving. We fantasized about dangerous driving with the tables unfolded. We loved all the things in the latched-down cupboards, exotic because they weren't the things we ate and drank with at home. We loved when the campervan roof got raised like a single wing; we fantasized about one day having that wing bit of the roof raised while we were on the road too.

Now Leif nosed the van off the dual carriageway, off the B road and down the smaller road that led home. This was a lane that the campervan was usually almost too big for. Tonight, though, the road seemed strange. It was wider.

What's happened here? Leif said. All the cow parsley gone.

A lot of the hedge growth and some of the bankage of the verges on either side had been roughly shoved back as if by bulldozer, earth and branches and leaves piled away against shorn shelves of foliage on either side of us.

Look at this, he said kicking away some rubble outside the front of our house on the pavement. What's this?

His boot was toeing a wedge of red colour next to our front gate.

It was a painted line.

His boot came away with a red smudge on the toe.

Someone had painted a line on the ground from where the side of our house met the next house on the terrace, the Upshaws' house, all the way round the outside of our house.

The red of the paint was bright on the tarmac.

Leif knocked on the Upshaws' front door. Mrs Upshaw didn't like people, she was just one of those people who didn't like people, capable from time to time of leaving a dead rat on top of the things in our bin to let us know we were on borrowed time as far as she was concerned. We didn't mind, nobody minded, we were happy, our mother always said, both to borrow and to lend what time we had while we could. Mr Upshaw did come to the door, though. He exchanged a glance with Leif about the red and then he and Leif stood talking like men do and pointing at the place where it stopped abruptly, where it met the Upshaws' property.

My sister touched the paint. She showed me the red that came off on her hands. Towards the back of the house where the tarmac turned into earth whoever had painted the red had simply laid the paint line over the loose bits of rubble, easily kicked or scraped away. I found a stick and scraped at it enough to make a gap. My sister walked through it like I'd made a door or a gate in it. She got the back door key out from underneath the shed and let us into the house.

I stood in the front room. Then I stood in the bedroom.

The rooms had a damp smell like we'd been away for years. Maybe this was just what it smelled like all the time and we'd stopped noticing. But the things in the house on the shelves, and even the actual furniture, looked like so much rubbish without our mother in the rooms.

So I went out and round the front again and stood in the garden leaning over the front gate. I watched Leif talking to Mr Upshaw. I watched his shoulders, and Mr Upshaw's shoulders. I could feel the grooved wood of the top of our front gate beneath my hand. What I thought of then was the dog we called Rogie, the stray that had lived with us for a while when I was small, he was a little dog, a wiry mongrel terrier. One day he'd been sitting by the campervan in the station car park when we came out of the cinema and it was very like he wanted a lift. So we gave him a lift, to ours, and he settled down in the kitchen and went to sleep straight away, slept the night there. After that he travelled into town with us whenever our mother drove in. We'd let him out in the car park, he'd run off to wherever he was going, we'd go and do whatever we were doing in town, then when we came back to the van he'd usually be there waiting for a lift back home. Then one day he didn't, he wasn't. He's moved on, our mother said, someone else'll be chauffeuring him now.

I thought how he'd been so clever on his feet that he could leap with ease this gate I was leaning on now, a gate five times taller than him. One spring evening our mother had shaken me awake, got me out of bed, carried me to the window and shown me him, poised, impossibly balanced on this narrow top rim of the gate here, all four paws tensed neat beside each other and his whole dog self tensed above them, steadying himself as he watched the comings and goings in the street, turned his head this way, that way, this way. He's been there like that for nearly twenty minutes, our mother said, I wanted you to see it.

When I felt the uneven wood under my hand now I thought of his clever eyes, his cocked ears, his moustachioed muzzle, how an armchair he'd been sleeping on kept his warmth still in it for a while after he jumped off. Then Leif said goodnight to Mr Upshaw, waved cheerily at the upstairs front window where Mrs Upshaw was watching behind her curtain, and knocked three times above the rust-tide on one of the orange sides of the campervan.

Everybody back in, he shouted. We're off. Where's your sister?

He went into the house to get her and came out carrying her in his arms across his chest. She was laughing.

Can I sit in the front? I said.

No, he said.

Can I? she said.

No, he said.

We seatbelted ourselves back in where we'd been, the seats still warm from us, and he took the blunt nose of the campervan down the changed lane, back out on to the road and away.

Who painted the red round our house? my sister said.

I wonder that too. But we'll probably never know, Leif said.

Was it people? she said.

Probably, one way or another, Leif said.

Why would people do that? she said.

People are people, Leif said, people are mysterious, why does anybody do anything?

Yeah but why are we leaving? I said.

It's time to, he said.

Where are we going? I said.

Where do you want to go? Leif said.

My sister and I, last summer, had seen something that happened to the place where people who travel up and down the country all year round and live in their vehicles usually parked and stayed for a while.

It was a grassy space between two roads, big enough for several caravans. The families who parked here usually came in June and left in July. They'd been doing this for longer than we'd been alive. Their children were our summer friends.

But last summer someone had filled that grassy space with massive jagged slabs of concrete, slanting and upright, slabs bigger than cars. My sister had burst into tears when she saw it. This was unlike her. She wasn't easily cowed.

Right now, strapped in next to me, she was pulling the arms and legs out of the doll she'd fished out of the ground in the back garden and shaking its torso so the small bits of rubble that were rattling about inside it would fall out, then poking it clean with the hem of her shirt before she pushed the bits of body back into their sockets.

Are we Travellers now? she said.

Yes, Leif said, that's what we're doing, we're travelling.

Good, I said, because then we'll see things all over again, and they'll be new, and the houses will look like they're different from normal houses.

We drove to a Tesco and parked at the top end of the car park. This was good because we'd have such easy access to shopping.

And it's a twenty four hour shop, Leif said, so with any luck they won't mind us being here overnight.

But in the middle of the night, still dark out, very early, I heard Leif turn over on the table-bed he and our mother slept on.

What is that sound? he said into the dark.

I sat up.

Lie down, Leif said. It'll just be wildlife.

But when we opened the door in the morning we saw that someone had painted a strip of red tightly round the edge of the campervan.

It went all the way round and met itself at the little metal step we'd left by the door for stepping safely out and in. The paint, still wet, was also on this step and a couple of the tyres and their wheel rims, even up the metalwork round the wheels.

We packed away the beds and the bed stuff and stowed the table and lowered the roof. We checked the latched cupboards to make sure they were ready for driving. My sister and I seatbelted ourselves in and I got myself at the exact right angle to see the painted outline of the campervan that'd be left behind us. Something in me was pleased that we'd leave this impression, in emergency red, the only bespoke van-shaped painted outline in the whole supermarket car park.

Leif put the key in the ignition and turned it. Nothing happened. He did it again. Nothing happened.

Then the towtruck came. While Leif argued with the security people we took the money he gave us and went into the supermarket.

We bought three loose croissants, made a coffee for him in a machine and bought as much cheese and ham as the woman behind the cold foods counter would give us for what change we had left. When we got back Leif'd taken everything we'd need out of the van and packed it into our rucksacks.

Mine was very light.

While the people fastened the towtruck hook somewhere the rust wouldn't give under the front of the campervan Leif lined all three of the croissants with the ham and the cheese the woman in the supermarket had sliced for us. He gave one croissant to me and one to my sister. He made one for himself, tore it in half, held the other half up and said,

this half's for your mother.

She's in another country, I said.

It'll be stale by the time she gets it, my sister said.

You best both eat it now, then, he said and he tore the half in half and gave us half of her half each.

We sat on the wall outside the supermarket and ate what we had. We watched the back of the campervan as it left the car park. I went to look at the red outline. When I came back I complained that the shape left by whoever'd painted round the campervan didn't look anything like the shape of a campervan.

Now we'll take that half a croissant belonging to her to your mother in the shape of you both, Leif said.

How will we? I said, now we've got no van?

We can ask for lifts to the port, he said. Then we can ask for lifts from the other port.

What if no one will give us a lift? I said.

Then we'll use our feet, he said.

All the way? I said.

What if she doesn't want us there because the art hotel doesn't allow people who aren't its guests in? my sister said.

They didn't even want us in that non-space they called the docking entrance, and what if she's not ready for us by the time we get there? I said.

Where will we live while we wait for her? my sister said.

We'll think of something, he said. I'll make some money. Your mother'll have been paid by then. We'll buy a new campervan.

But what if they paint a line round you, or round us, round our feet, or even on to our feet, at the port? my sister said. Or before we get to the port? What if it happens any minute now, what if we walk out on to the road and we're trying to work out which way to go to get to the port and people, whoever, just run at us out of nowhere with a paintbrush? What if they paint it right over my shoes?

What bright red shoes you'll have if anyone does that thing to you, Leif said.

We took a train to another town. It wasn't far but Leif said it was far enough. All the way there Leif sat saying nothing in the window seat where the sun glint was so bright that if I looked at him it hurt my eyes.

When we arrived and came through the barriers and out and were standing in the sun waiting for him to tell us where we were going he said he'd been thinking hard and coming to a conclusion and now he'd decided something.

No! we both said at once.

We want to come too, my sister said.

Why can't we? I said.

It'll be easier, he said. Think about it. I can travel lighter if we do this and be back here with her sooner.

It was true that we'd spent hours in rooms at the

various borders and ports and airports *for our own good* while people in uniforms in other rooms verified Leif because him travelling with us and us travelling with him and him and us not being related was suspicious enough to mean you tended to have to miss flights and ships, unless you were very rich and could pass through border control without having to be so verified.

You're slaking us off like a snake sheds a skin off, my sister said.

Not slaking, I said. Shaking. Or sloughing.

She started singing the words *snake it off, snake it off*, to the tune of the old song called Shake It Off.

Are you calling me a snake? Leif said. He made both his arms go snaky and his hands be like snake mouths while he himself pretended not to notice what his own arms were doing.

Neither of us laughed.

Are we going to have to stay somewhere with people we don't know? I said.

He dropped his arms to his sides.

Well, I have an idea, he said.

We stood in the station car park while he phoned someone who knew someone who had a house in this town we might be able to live in.

But what if the people who don't think we should be allowed come here and find us when you're not here? my sister said.

They won't, Leif said.

How do you know? I said.

How will they know where you are? he said. Or who you are?

But what if whoever looks after us tells them who and where we are? I said.

That won't happen because nobody will be looking after you, because you'll be looking after yourselves, he said.

Oh, I said.

Will we? my sister said.

I think you're old enough now and responsible enough to do this for a short time, he said.

We are, I said. I am.

Will you tell our mother where we're staying when we get to the new place? my sister was saying.

What do you think? Leif said.

Yeah, what do you think? I said too.

Even so my stomach was turning over on itself inside me.

On our walk over to the new place he stopped and went into a corner shop to get something from someone. We sat outside on the kerb and waited.

Leif is leaving us, my sister said.

Not for long, I said.

I said it to my stomach.

Leif is leaving, she said.

I shook my head at her like I was annoyed with her and she was being annoying.

But maybe she was right, maybe he was leaving us, all of us, including our mother. Maybe he wouldn't be back at all. Maybe he would travel so light that no trace of him would remain anywhere and that would be Leif gone out of our life. Then maybe our mother, if she came home, when she did, by herself, would have no idea we'd moved and would go to the place that had last been our home but we wouldn't be there, we'd be somewhere she'd no idea about and we'd have no idea about her.

If he doesn't come back, I said, we'll phone her.

We don't have a phone, she said. She doesn't either.

We'll ask someone if we can borrow theirs for a minute and we'll tell them we'll pay for the call and we'll call Alana's phone, I said.

I said Alana's number to myself inside my head. And if Alana's phone isn't working or nobody answers it, I thought without saying anything out loud, we'll leave a message. And we'll phone the art hotel. And we can go back on the train, it's only half an hour on the train, if we need to, and tell the Upshaws, in case she goes there looking for us, and maybe they might, he might, tell her.

I sat and thought of more and more things to do and ways to do them. The things and ways spread out round me like the nets trapeze artists up in the roofs of circus tents had beneath the tightropes and trapezes in case they fell.

Leif is leaving, Leif is leaving, my sister was saying under her breath in a sing-song next to me, hitting one of her heels quite hard against the kerb to keep time with herself saying it.

Leif came out of the shop with four plastic bags filled with tins. He told us he'd calculated what we'd need for each meal, including for breakfasts. He didn't think it'd take nearly as long as the number of tins he'd bought, but he'd bought, just in case, exactly how many it would take for the longest length of time it *could* take for him to get there and bring her back. Plus, he'd bought this. He moved all the bags to one hand, put his other hand in his jacket pocket and held up a new tin opener.

Just as well he had because the house was empty. I mean there was nothing, not even any cupboards or drawers you could put tins or a tin opener into and no furniture anywhere in it at all. He opened its front door and we ran in making the sound an empty place makes with people in it, all three of us both bigger and smaller at once on the floorboards and up and down the wooden stairs, our voices booming when we called to each other from room to room. There were more than enough rooms. There were three upstairs and three downstairs not including the little hall. We'd never been in a house with so many. Only the place where we'd left our coats on the wooden post at the end of the stairs and our bags on the floor beneath them sounded a bit more like somewhere normal, if we stood quite near our things when we spoke.

Leif went round the house from room to room. He flicked each light switch in each room. We have power! he said when the first light switch worked. The lightbulbs lit up the nothing in the rooms and the mild pink colour of the walls with no paper or paint on them. Upstairs there was a toilet. It was old and its ceramic underneath was broken. Leif checked it. It worked. There was a bath, newer, cleaner. Its taps worked. There was a sink with taps that worked. The water was cold. Downstairs in a room at the back of the house there was a bigger sink. The water was cold there too.

Leif took the little kettle he'd bought out of its plastic and filled it with water. He plugged it in. It worked.

And there's a bit of a garden at the back, he said as he pulled his jacket on at the front door.

He got some keys out of his pocket and showed them to us.

This little key must be the back door one. This is the front door yale, look. This is the mortice.

He gave me the keys and shouldered his rucksack. He took a roll of cash with an elastic band round it out of his inside jacket pocket and held it out to me too.

But we'll be back well before the tins run out, he

said. So we'll want this cash back unspent, if possible. I know how good you are with money.

We came outside with him on to the street's pavement and he closed the door behind us. It locked us out by itself on the yale.

Now you open it, he said to me.

He watched while I did. Then he closed it again and told me to double lock it then to open it again, this time with both keys. Then he made my sister do the same thing, though I made it pretty clear it'd be me who'd be in charge of the keys.

He opened his arms.

Be good, you two, he said.

We stood outside the locked door and watched him till he got to the end of the road. He turned and waved. We waved too till he'd completely gone and we were waving at nothing but the bend in the road and the corrugated iron fenced-off place at the dead end of this street.

Then I stood looking at the street with him not in it for a bit just to get used to it and to where we were and also to dare myself to be a bit visible, see what happened if I did on this new street. I sat on the house's low front wall and looked up the street then the other way too like I always lived here and was surveying my lot, as our mother put it when she sat taking everything in like this.

I got even braver. I took a walk up and down this bit of the street.

There was no red paint round any house near us that I could see.

Maybe the red paint thing was only specific to the place we used to live, not here. I checked all the houses' outsides where their fronts or their gates met the pavement. Then I checked between and round the parked cars. The houses had wildly varying different sizes of front garden or front drive. Some on the other side had quite big front spaces, big enough, some, for a campervan even, while some had almost no space at all, like the space we had behind this wall I was now back sitting on again, which you couldn't have called a front garden or a front anything, just two concrete slabs, hardly even enough room for my sister to do what she was now doing.

She was acting like someone five years younger than she was, crouching down then springing up with her arms stretched out, crouching down then springing up and throwing out her arms.

I told her to stop it.

I'll starjump if I like wherever I like whenever I like, she said.

All the same she stopped. She said,

he didn't say he'd be back soon.

But he will, I said. He inferred it.

Inferred, inferred, she sang and crouched and starjumped knocking her arm against the little wall each time.

You'll skin your elbow, I said.

She said she was doing what she was doing to keep warm because she was cold. I told her to grow up. But the sun had come off the front of the house and I was quite cold now too. Then a man walking past the house looked up from his phone, looked at us hard and held his phone up, so I got the keys out of my pocket. Instead of looking at the man looking at us through his phone I studied the keyring the keys were all fixed to. It was the see-through plastic window type and had a photograph of somebody else's children in it.

I unlocked the door no problem. I locked it from the inside with the mortice key like Leif had said. I got the money he'd given me out, took the elastic band off it and counted it then I rolled it back up again and put it in my pocket with the keys.

Our duffelcoats and rucksacks were still there in the hall. It wasn't too cold in this house yet. The front door was a very nice old one, shining varnished wood except for the letterbox down low and the slice of glass down the middle of the door, the kind of glass you can't see clearly through but that still lets in the light. The tin opener was still on the windowsill in the room with the big sink which Leif had said was the kitchen. The forty two tins were in here, arranged in a pyramid on the floor.

Thirty six meatballs in tomato sauce, four creamed rice, two sweetcorn. If we ate six tins a day, one each for each meal, that meant the probable longest time they'd be away was seven days from now. But maybe Leif had calculated that my sister would only eat half a tin each time. Let's say he'd calculated I'd eat a whole tin. Seven days meant twenty one for me and half that number for her. That left ten and a half tins over. If together we ate four and a half tins each day then that meant an extra possible two days to add on to the seven, plus one meal each the following day, so, say, three extra days in all. Which made a possible ten days at the longest. Though if we both only ate half a tin each per meal that made it longer, more like a fortnight.

I resolved to eat a whole tin every time.

But what if, if I did, we ran out?

What if Alana still wasn't better after a fortnight?

Or what if it took until September?

It was now only just April.

Leif is leaving. Leif is leaving.

I picked up the tin opener. I picked up one of the tins.

My sister was standing next to me now so close I could feel her breath on my arm.

You hungry? I said.

She shook her head. She put her mouth against my T-shirt shoulder and breathed her breath warm into it like she used to when she was smaller.

Me neither, I said. So we won't eat yet. So, what we'll do now is, we'll choose our favourite room.

Favourite room for what? she said.

For eating and sleeping in, I said. For instance, you can sleep in the bath. And in the morning I can wake you up by turning on the taps.

She laughed.

No, *you* can sleep in the bath, she said.

We can both sleep in the bath, I said. One at either end. You at the uncomfortable end with the taps.

No, *you* for instance, she said, *you*.

She was laughing.

And then I'll tell you a story, I said. No, I know. You can tell me one. You're better at it than me.

What about?

That's not up to me, I said. That'll be up to you. So. What'll it be about?

I don't know yet, she said.

When will you know?

How will I know till I'm making it up? she said.

Next morning, first light, my sister was asleep with her head on my legs and her duffelcoat over her including her head. I didn't want to wake her so I lay there for a while not moving. Then when my own head on my rucksack got uncomfortable I sat up slow, folded back the duffelcoat, lifted her head while I shifted then let it as gently as I could back down on to my shins. She snorted in her sleep but she didn't waken. One of her hands tightened round my ankle.

I looked at where the green colour of the edge of my own duffelcoat under us met the black lines running between the floorboards. The black lines weren't black lines at all. They were thin spaces, narrow air cracks between the nailed-down planks.

These houses were once railwaymen's cottages, Leif had told us, his voice massive in the nothing.

They were built, he said, *by* people building the railways, *for* people building the railways. In other words for themselves to live in while they did the work. They were probably meant to be temporary houses. It'd probably amaze them that they've lasted so long. They'll have used their everyday building materials to make them. These boards under our feet were probably originally sleepers to be used on railway lines under the rails.

Funny now to think of us and of all the people before us who'd ever lived in this house asleep on something called sleepers.

I'd seen yesterday on one of the houses in this terrace a date above a door. 1868. These houses would have housed a lot of people over all those years. What was left now of the people who'd lived here was down there, had fallen between the boards over time, dust etc, along with bits of spiders' legs and webs, shells of woodlice and long gone ladybirds, layered over by what was left of the next people, then the next, and so on all the way up to us here now.

Our mother had once taken us to visit what she said was a famous battlefield. It was just a field, just grass for miles. She'd stood with us one on either side of her, held our hands and said,

can you feel all the people here and what happened to them?

No, we said.

Try harder, she said.

I reached and slid a finger along one of the spaces between the boards. If you could take these boards up and look at what had ended up down there in that under-the-boards space it'd look like just dirt and grime. But you'd not just have DNA galore, you'd have the *actual matter* of what was left of those people and their times. This was a completely different sort of matter, the kind people say doesn't matter when they talk about what history is.

I felt beneath the hood of my coat for the house's keys. Still there. I looked at the photo of the happy children in the window of the keyring. They were maybe some of the people who used to live here when there were household goods and things in it making it lived-in. Bright colour in the photo. A garden. Maybe this house's back garden? We hadn't yet gone out to look at any garden; last night we'd been being as good and quiet as secret mice, we'd chosen this room upstairs at the front as the best to take all our things into, including the tins, the tin opener and the kettle, and we'd left the light off so we wouldn't inadvertently draw attention to ourselves by a light being on in an empty house. We'd moved around between upstairs and downstairs being as silent as we could then we'd sat close together on the floor in this corner of the room, eaten here and fallen asleep here.

It didn't look old, the photo of the children.

It looked like a picture more or less from now, could've been taken right now if it weren't a photo, which obviously immediately placed the people it was of in a past. There were three, all roughly the same age as me or maybe a bit older, all lying on their fronts on grass that looked like lawn and smiling at the camera. There were trees above them at the sides of the photo and a blue sky directly above so bright that it turned the grass nearer them colourless. Two with dark hair, one with yellow hair. They were wearing T-shirts and they were posing in a row the same way as each other for the photo, all leaning on the grass on their elbows with their chins cupped in their hands.

Maybe the person who owned or rented this house had given Leif this keyring with their picture in it so Leif wouldn't forget that it wasn't his house and that they'd want it back.

Or maybe the family of the people in the photo had moved elsewhere and that's why the house was available for us to use.

I could go back to the shop where Leif got the keys and ask the person or people behind the counter if these children were their children.

My sister shifted, said something in her sleep, turned over, stayed asleep.

She was so smart. I knew what she would say if I were to say any of this to her out loud. *They're nothing to do with us or here. And even if they were. We're here now.* She'd say something like *they're not even real children. They're AI. They never existed.* Or *obvs you loser it's a picture of people who were chosen because they look right, they're people who didn't even know each other having their picture taken by some photographer who didn't know them either and then the photographer sold it to a conlomerate.* She always missed out the g in conglomerate. I said she did this because she didn't know how to say it, she said it was because she was taking some of a conlomerate's power away from it by mis-saying it. *And then machines made a lot of copies of the same photo and inserted them into a lot of keyrings so that these keyrings would sell to people who saw them wherever, in shops or online, by giving people the idea that they could put their own kids' photo in there.*

It was quite usual and acceptable now for photos that purported to be true pictures of reality not to be what they were or appeared to be.

All the old photos of our mother at our age, photos before phone photos, were definitely unaltered and of undisguised real realities, and were kept in a box under her bed at home.

Inside that box she also kept the necklace, real pearls, that her mother's mother had given her daughter and so on down the line. I liked it when we looked at the photos in the box because it was an excuse to try the necklace on. It looked really good no matter what you wore. It looked especially good with clothes that weren't the kind of clothes you'd usually wear a necklace like that one with. It looked great, for instance, with a shirt and tie, twice round the neck then under the collar and running tucked under the tie.

I really liked how it looked and how I looked in it.

My sister's head and shoulders felt heavy on me now. I looked across the room at the line of tins we'd placed against the far wall. Which would we open for breakfast? We'd agreed last night that we'd always keep the creamed rice for only really great days.

The children in that keyring photo looked like they were having a really great day.

There was no such thing as AI children. You were either an alive one, or someone who'd once been a child and was now older, or a dead one; even if the children in the photo *were* advertising models – which did seem most likely the more I thought about it – then they were still children, or they'd been children *once*. Well, provided they weren't invented by a computer collating thousands of digital images down into one single child then another and another, people who'd never existed.

Even so, even the thousands of fragments of images AI would use to make a non-existent child had to have come from children who'd been complete children *once*.

Where were they now? All of them, the maybe-real ones cupping their chins so happily here in the sun in the photo *and* all those ones whose images had been fragmented into digital splinters and borrowed and used to make up an aggregate image of a child who'd never existed.

What were they doing in the world at this precise moment, the people these maybe-real children had become *and* the people the thousands of splintered borrowed children had become?

I could trace our path back to the station and buy a return ticket (I had money, if they still took cash at the station) and walk to the house and sneak in and get our old family photos.

I could bring the necklace too for safe keeping.

I could bring back the wildflower book our mother had given me with its handpainted illustrations.

I knew much of it by heart.

Stonecrop, a mossy herb, so called for its ability to grow itself out of nothing but rock and stone, likes nothing better than a wall or stony place.

Campion is any of many plants of the genera, with pink, white or red flowering, its name arising from the word champion, possibly from an old tradition of its leaves being used for garlands for champions.

I could also get our mother's laptop. I knew where she hid it. I knew her passwords.

I would go through the cupboard in the big bedroom and try and find one of the old phones and its charger. Then we'd have a phone of sorts.

Our mother thought smartphones were *liabilities*. So, what you want, she'd say whenever we begged her for a smartphone or a smart anything, is to have a device that means you see everything through it, as if everything is at your fingertips and you can hold it all in the palm of one hand. It would certainly make you feel very important to yourself. What you'd be preoccupied with would be so important to you that there would be no point in you looking at anything else.

She refused to have one herself, barely put up with Leif having one. She told us that her generation, when she was very small, had been prepared for smartphones by a craze for tiny toy machine-creatures that fitted into the palm of a hand. You brought them to life by pressing an on button, then after you did you had to feed, water and attend to them at many different times of the day and if you didn't do this enough times then the machine-creatures died. Their mouths turned down and their eyes were replaced by an x and an x.

And that's what people, somewhere in their unconscious, think about their smartphones, she said, that if they don't keep attending to them and pressing their buttons, always making them light up and answering every little baby chicken automated cheep they make, then there's sure to be a death, but this time it'll be you, the owner of the phone, that'll be a new kind of dead. Later in life you'll thank me for protecting you from these liabilities.

Thank you or tank you? my sister said.

What does that mean, tank me? she said.

You'll never know unless you look it up on a phone or a laptop, I said.

She shook her head at us.

There are different realities, she'd say, and the net is a reality with designs on general reality, and I'll prefer it if you both experience the real realities as your foremost realities.

You are denying us the education that most kids our age are getting from their devices, I said.

No I'm not, she said. Truthfully I'm amazed anyway that you in particular, Bri, seem to know, without anyone ever telling you, how to make devices do what you want them to do. But I'm asking you to source your education more widely and more dimensionally.

AI is a fantastic thing that has even made it possible for us to read the scrolls that were burnt closed and before would just fall apart if you tried to open them into nothing but ashes in that volcano place called Herculaneum, I said.

If only people paid more attention, she said, to

what history tells us rather than all this endless congratulating ourselves for finding a new way to read it.

All the ways of reading are good, I said.

She agreed.

But she said she could remember a time not so long ago when the word social had meant something very different, and that social media could do all sorts of good things but that too many people – and more, too many powerful systems – used it vindictively.

I'd asked her if I could look up on her laptop what social and vindictively meant and she'd laughed and said go to the library and look them up, and I said, okay, take me to a town that still has a library and I'll look them up on a library computer then, you do know that libraries are mostly computers now, and she'd said God help me, what can one woman do against the behemoth, here, go on, look up the word behemoth, and handed me her laptop with a search page open, though she still waited with me and supervised me the whole time I looked it up, and laughed and put her arm round me when I was surprised by a behemoth not actually being a kind of moth.

Maybe there were new people in our house now.

Maybe someone had emptied our house of all our stuff.

Maybe our home looked like this house now.

Maybe new people were filling it with their stuff.

Maybe people who'd been marked out with red paint were only allowed houses like this one, with nothing in it, so we didn't forget we were that word temporary.

If these children in the photo *were* real, and *were* people who used to live here, had they been made to move all their stuff so people who'd had the red paint treatment could live here?

I could go to that shop where Leif got the keys. I could ask them there where I could find a phone shop, the kind that unlocks phones, where someone might be more persuaded to sell me a phone without proof of age. It had said on a poster I'd seen in Tesco that you could get a really good new pay as you go deal if you were eighteen. Someone at a phone unlocking shop could probably be persuaded to do a cheap discreet deal with someone underage.

I could see if they had a laptop too in that phone shop, one that they'd sell me cheap. If they took cash. Sure they'd take cash, that kind of shop still did, and there were lots of places where you could get online for free. Station ticket office. They'd have it free there probably.

I started making a list.

Phone.

Online access, free.

Fork and spoon each: any fast food place, free.

Weapon of some kind.

Way to make money.

Bike for getting to places faster if need be. Some wheel sizes of bike were definitely faster than others. Were some colours of bike faster than others? Our bikes would be long gone by now. Someone else would be riding my light blue bike really fast round our neighbourhood.

I could go and check in case. Maybe nobody'd thought to look in our shed.

Had the people who'd lived here while they were building the railway got up and gone to work at the station on foot or on bikes from the past? Were the bikes then like bikes are now, or were they the penny farthing type?

When I got us a laptop I'd look up a bike timeline.

But would people who worked on railways be the kind of people who had bikes or would that only be rich people in 1868? Those bikes from the past were generally dark colours. Or was I thinking this because old style photos made it falsely look like the world didn't do colours back then? And had the people who lived here not only built the railway but also built the station, I mean built the building where the ticket office was, the high-ceilinged one we were in yesterday with Leif? Imagine if we were now in one place and yesterday we'd been in a quite other place and these two places which were nothing like each other and didn't seem connected to each other by anything had in fact something really essential in common. Imagine what it'd be like if we could see or know or feel or sense like by some sense more than the senses we already had corre spon dence s that were other wise total all y fore ver in vis

When I woke up it was because my sister was shouting at me from the door of the room.

Come *on*, she was shouting. You won't *believe* it.

I heard her run downstairs.

I sat up.

Money still in my pocket?

Yes.

Keys –

There was an imprint of the keyring in the skin of my hand where I'd been holding the keys in my sleep.

I got up, looked under the coats. I looked in all my pockets and shook out our coats and rucksacks.

I'd only had the keys one day and I'd lost them already.

Downstairs the front door was still closed and locked. But there was outside air coming into the house from somewhere.

I went through the main rooms and into the room with the big low sink in it. The back door was unbolted, hanging open. The keyring was still swinging slightly from the key in its lock.

The back garden lawn was a steep slant of grass tipped up on its side like a sinking ship. There were stone slabs, then at the end of them this wedge of grass so steep it was like the world had upended.

At the top of it was an overgrown hedge and a lot of ivy.

But there was a gap in this hedge and footholds in the grassy slant that led to the gap so I worked my way up it and bent myself low enough to squeeze through, out on to the surprise of a public footpath. It was the paved kind with a line of grass running up the middle of it. Across this, across a busy traffic road and across another scrubland, my sister in the distance, I knew her by her clothes, was perched up on one of the struts of a wooden fence and leaning over its top.

When I got there she turned to me and her face was full of happiness.

Look at what there is so close to where we live! she said.

I climbed up on to the fence too.

Seven horses, small and large, all the colours of horse, beautiful and mangy, were drifting their noses across grass and ripping it with their teeth from the ground making a sound I'd never heard before.

Can we go and get some of our food and give them it? she said.

Horses don't eat food that comes in tins, I said.

What do they eat? she said.

Grass, I said, and other stuff. Not tinned stuff.

She jumped back down off the fence and scrambled about pulling handfuls of the longer grass on our side of it. She got back up on the fence and held it out with both her hands.

Two of the horses lifted their heads, a broad dark brown one with a white stripe down its nose and a smaller grey-coloured one. She waved the grass at them. The grey one came over. Its head moved up and down as it walked and I realized that though we'd seen horses in books and on TV and passed quite close to them abroad, blinkered and sweating and pulling decorated carriages carrying tourists through traffic, I'd truly never been this near a freed-up horse.

I'd never smelled one either. The smell was deep and hearty and unlike anything I knew.

The grey horse's bones were close to its skin all over it and it seemed huge even though it was quite a small horse, the smallest one in this field. It moved with laidback strength and with a real weightiness though it wasn't weighty at all, it was as spare as a bare tree. It stopped close to my sister leaning towards it over the fence. Flies hung around its head, landed on its forehead, a strangely flattened place, the horsehair on it under its forelock going in a whorl like it was marking an important place on a horse.

It had a line of lighter grey jagged like lightning down its nose and the flies round its head kept landing near its eye, maybe for a drink because the eye shone like a liquid source.

The eye was shocking.

It was really beautiful.

You could see light in its dark, and it also had in it, both at once, two things I had never seen together in one place, gentleness, and – what?

Politeness? Indifference? Distance?

I won't know the word for it till now, years after, right this minute, walking to wherever in the dark and permitting myself to think back to the moment I first ever saw, so close to my own eyes, any horse's, this horse's, eye.

The word is equanimity.

My sister was holding the grass out in her two clenched fists. The horse stood. It waited. Then it nudged one of her arms with its long face and nosed the back of her hand round and down.

Oh, she said. Oh. Right.

She opened her hand and it took the grass, the horse took it!

She did the same with her other hand open even flatter. It took it. It watched us while it ate it with its big loose jaw moving.

The smell of the grass getting eaten filled the air round us with a strange sweetness.

We had an argument back at the house about whether or not giving a horse in a field some grass to eat for the first time made this the kind of day we could open one of the creamed rice tins for breakfast.

I can't believe you're saying no when we can do what we like, there is nobody here to stop us and it's what I want and choose to eat, my sister said.

Her happiness had started to annoy me. So I said, I can't believe you're being so profligate already.

Being so what? she said.

Profligate, I said.

You are bullying me with words longer than the length of my life, she said.

It's not my problem if you don't know what words mean, I said.

What I know is we just had the best thing happen

to us that we've had happen to us for weeks, she said, probably one of the best things that *will* happen for ages.

There are only four tins of creamed rice, I said.

So? she said.

So we have to ration them, I said.

Why? she said.

Because we agreed that we'd keep them for the best days, I said.

Yeah and this is one of the best mornings in my whole life! she said.

But not simultaneously one of mine, I said and felt churlish and superior as I said it.

I simultaneously hate you, she said.

And I find you unsupportive and insupportable, I said.

You are so up yourself, she said.

You don't know what that phrase really means, I said.

Yes I do, she said.

And you always have to have the last word, I said.

No I don't, she said.

Any other time she'd have realized that what she was doing, saying that, was having the last word and she'd have burst out laughing and so would I and something would have given way between us.

Today for some reason that didn't happen. What did happen was that neither of us ate anything at all that morning for breakfast. She went upstairs.

I thought she was making for the rice tins so I followed her but she didn't even look at them, went straight to our duffelcoats instead and sat on both of them mounded up, pulling the legs out of her doll and marching the legless torso up and down the mounds of duffel singing something to herself or to it.

I stood in the doorway with my face solemn.

I'm going out, I said. There's several important things I have to do. I'm delegating the looking-after of this house to you till I get back and I need you to be responsible. Do you hear me?

She carried on singing as if I wasn't there.

Right, I said. I'm going now. I'm going to lock the doors. You are now solely responsible till I get back.

She carried on singing.

Be quiet. Be quieter, I said.

She stopped for a moment and looked right at me. All her ways of listening to music were lost now back in our old house. I felt bad. But I went downstairs anyway. As I went, her singing started up again and got louder and angrier and by the time I pulled the front door towards me to double lock it I could hear her charging about in the upstairs front room sing-shouting and dancing a thumping dance on the bare boards.

I went the same way round the corner that Leif had gone and walked down one of the roads we'd taken yesterday.

I was hungry. But there was no way I was going to break into our cash for something as dilettante as breakfast for myself when we had tins we were meant to eat from that I could open when I got home.

Whenever we were hungry our mother'd say *ah but wait and I'll make us all something very grand.*

You took two slices of bread and you buttered them. You took two spring onions and you removed the sprout ends and the very ends of the green bits. If the onion wasn't clean you could also slit into it and slip off its top coat. Then you chopped the rest up quite fine. You sprinkled the chopped onions on one of the slices of bread and added salt and pepper then put the other slice on top and cut the whole thing into four.

Now I was thinking about what a spring onion sandwich tasted like, tangy and buttery at once.

We can't solve it. But we can still salve it.

That was something else our mother'd say.

When I got back to our old house I'd look for and bring my sister her earbuds and the old player she played her music with.

If they were still there.

If whoever was in there now, if anyone was, hadn't sold them or wasn't using them in their own ears.

I recognized the corner shop where Leif had bought the tins.

I went in.

But I didn't want to spend any money and the people behind the counter looked at me as soon as I came in like I was going to steal something and one of them came out from behind the counter and started following me round the shop. So I left.

I found the station.

I went in.

I was going back home.

But to get a ticket I'd need someone to buy it on a card for me because there was no one there to take cash and only machines that didn't take cash and there were signs everywhere about how much I'd be fined if I got on a train without a ticket. The fine was for more money than Leif had given us.

Also, according to the machine where I keyed in our home town as a destination, a return ticket was going to cost me nearly half of our money.

I stood outside again in the place we'd stood yesterday when Leif had told us he was leaving us. Across the road a man in red overalls was pushing what looked like a lawnmower with a large plastic container balanced on top of it along the pavement outside an old building. An elderly woman in a long black coat was following him and shouting at him.

You can't bulldoze history, she was shouting.

Doing my job, he was saying. What I'm paid to. Don't mess with me.

Don't do this, she was saying.

Back off, he said. I'm warning you.

You've got a choice, she said.

It belongs to the people who've bought it, he said. They decide, not me. Not you, lady.

A small crowd of people had gathered in a semicircle to watch them. I crossed the road and stood watching too.

Not a lawnmower. It was a strange machine.

It had one thick wheel and a network of plastic piping below the big container which was fitted with a funnel. It had words on its side, the name of its make.

SUPERA BOUNDER.

The machine looked like an invention made by

an amateur for a joke. The red paint line it left behind it on the pavement was a thick one and shining, still wet.

But the woman was standing in front of him now, she was holding the front of the supera bounder machine to stop it. He leaned on its handle pushing hard back at her. Now he was swearing at her, calling her a bag of bones.

Oh a charming man, she said and someone in the group of people stifled a laugh.

She heard it. Still blocking the supera bounder she turned her head to appeal to us, shunted one of her shoulders against the front of it like it took nothing out of her at all, held up her other arm like a person conversing while doing a magic trick and said,

listen, I'm seventy nine, I've a lifetime's worth of experience in the pushy tactics of men and what he doesn't know yet is I can keep this up all day *and* night.

A semicircle of laughs.

Still, I could do with a cigarette break if anyone'd like to take over and hold him at bay for the next three minutes, she said.

Nobody in the crowd moved.

No? she said.

She returned her whole weight to the machine, was still holding him off but now her body was beginning to shake with the effort of it.

Then the man pushing the supera bounder let go of the handle very suddenly and dodged to the side so the machine juddered away from her, the woman fell forward and as she fell he darted at her, rugby tackled her and knocked her sideways away from the supera bounder. She rolled on to the pavement, and so did the man, and the supera bounder rolled off course quite fast right towards me leaving a line of red behind it.

I threw my weight at the side of it as hard as I could. It was heavier than it looked. It balanced on the side of its wheel for a moment as if deciding. I kicked it. The kick tipped it over. The wheel came off. The funnel fell off.

Voluminous redness spilled out of the top of the huge container. It flowed down towards me – I dodged out of its way – and curdled all round the base of a traffic light pole, dripping off the kerb. The people nearest it on the pavement backed off fast. The traffic light changed. A woman on a bike guided her bike round the red like it had always been there. Drivers in passing traffic saw it and began swerving to avoid getting it on their wheels.

The man in overalls pushed the elderly woman up off him and stumbled to his feet. He was yelling. He ran towards the upturned supera bounder shouting the word NO.

Meanwhile I'd placed myself next to another man as if I were with him. He'd let me do this by acting as if he didn't notice me. Then I slipped in next to a woman, then next to two boys, I didn't catch anyone's eye, nobody caught mine and nobody gave me away. I ducked round the back of all the standing people and walked off openly as if I had no idea what was happening and was a person on my way home from somewhere totally other, right past the man in overalls who hadn't seen what happened and was shrieking now about losing his job.

When I'd got as far as the corner behind a large van I rounded it and stood in a closed shop doorway where I checked myself over, my hands, feet, clothes.

I used an old car's wing mirror to check my face and head.

Then I set off back to the house fast, my feet keeping time with my heart.

So, yes. There *was* red painting round things here, too.

Supera boundering.

Had someone pushed a supera bounder like that one round the outside of our house and garden?

Who?

I felt suddenly like I might be sick.

Had someone, whoever they were, in the middle of the night, pushed such a stupid looking apparatus that close to us all in the campervan, us asleep?

They'd arrived, they'd scoped it. They'd have had to re-aim its nozzle to get as close to us as they did.

Who did that, re-aimed the plastic nozzle? Who filled the big container with the paint? Who told them to, and paid them to?

Who took money – *doing my job* – for doing, with that ridiculous looking machine, that ridiculous thing to us?

Never mind, never mind. I knew this town a bit now. I knew now how to get from one place to another in it, *and* back again. You always had to be careful to know how to get back again, sometimes by different routes or means. I already knew this just from everyday living and being my age; it didn't take some supera bounder machine to teach me it.

When I got back there, if the house hadn't burnt down with her in it – and she was capable of producing smoke and fire from nothing, I was sure – I'd go straight upstairs and get the tin opener from where I'd hidden it. I'd give it and one of the tins of creamed rice to my sister. I'd say, go on, open it. I'd say sorry, I'd say –

There was a hand on my shoulder. A quiet voice behind me.

Wait for me, you little revolutionary.

Hello, she said and she passed me as if leaning on a stranger's shoulder for a passing moment was what an elderly lady would do just to stay upright and keep walking if she happened to be passing someone, a momentary support, nothing personal.

She sailed ahead in the flow of her long black coat.

Hello, I said to the back of the coat.

I'm Oona, she said ahead of me without turning her head.

Then she said,

can you hear me back there?

Yes. Pleased to meet you, I said.

How polite, she said. Jolly nice. No, stay back there, don't keep up with me, walk behind me. Pretend we don't know each other.

We don't, I said.

Quite right, she said. And don't look up, but

can you see the camera on the top of the post on the right, the one we're coming towards? When I stop speaking we're at the end of the distance to and from a camera in this part of town where what you're saying can be heard, and when we pass it and I start speaking again we're back at the start.

She stopped speaking. We walked a bit further. She started speaking again.

Speak low when you do speak. The mikes on these poles aren't as powerful as the ones in the town centre but they're still miked up. Got that?

Yes, I said.

Okay, she said, we're all right for twenty yards. Now. I told you my name. You haven't told me your name.

Briar, I said

Briar, she said. You don't seem the overly thorny type to me.

You don't know me, I said.

Yet, she said.

Oona is also a quite notable name, I said.

Again, how polite you are, she said.

I was called after a song, I said, that our mother likes, it's got a rose in it and a briar and she wanted them both, so I have a sister and my sister's called Rose.

A rose and a briar, she said. And your mother got you both. I think I might know that song.

It's got a couple in it and one loves the other but the other doesn't love them back –

Tell me the rest in a moment, I'll say when.

[Pause.]

Tell me now, she said.

Okay so then the one who loves but who is unrequited goes and dies and gets buried and the one left behind realizes they're heartbroken and that they really did love the dead person, so they die too, and they both get buried in the same churchyard and out of the ground where the first one is buried a rose grows and out of the other one a briar, and the flowers grow up the churchyard wall and they sort of tie themselves together even though the dead people they're growing out of missed their chance.

Yes, the woman called Oona said. Thought so. Very old ballad.

Walking ahead of me in the street in her long black coat which flapped on one side like a black wing, she sang.

In Scarlet Town, where I was born

There was a fair maid dwelling.

That one? she said.

I don't know it, I said. I only know there's a briar and a rose and they grow up a tall wall and over it and go as high as they can go, all interwoven with each other.

Piece of pure historical gender-pressurizing, Oona said.

Is it? I said.

Given that the woman in it has to learn her lesson, she said, because she didn't love him when he was alive, so now she has to die too, and of all the things she has to die of, she has to die of love. Load of rot.

I don't think our mother knew that about that song, I said. When she chose it.

I hope not, the woman called Oona said. But imagine if one day a songwriter had the talent enough to write a song solely about two beautiful plants that grow together, one cultivated, one wild, up and over a wall. With no human inference at all to be taken from it. Except that plants growing up and over a wall are very fine things in themselves. Tell her when you get home I hope she called you it because you're thorny enough never to be bullied to death like the person in that song.

Oh, yes. I will, I said.

Where's home, when you're at home?

I made something up. I told her my whole family lived a forty minute walk from here.

I'm going that way too, she said. We'll go together.

Were you called Oona for a reason like a song? I said.

It's because I'm the one and the only, she said. And simultaneously universal. No, I'm actually named after a grandmother. Though sure enough that grandmother was also the one and the only, and the universal. Also a goddess. Do you believe me?

I'll reserve judgement for now if you don't mind and tell you later in our relationship, I said.

She laughed out loud for real. Then she pretended with her whole body to be an old person just having a memory that had made her laugh. We passed another camera pole, her moving at her steady pace which was surprisingly fast, quite hard to keep up with, so I pretended I was playing a jumping game not standing on the cracks, which let me vary my pace.

Then she asked me if I'd mind telling her whether I'd knocked it over by accident, or because I was brave, or because I was an innocent.

All three of those, I said.

Witty with it, she said. But – and now I'm being serious. Be careful after today. CC will have caught and stored what happened today. They'll facially trail you now.

They'll trail you too, I said. More.

Oh, I'm a trained elusive, she said.

Can I ask something?

Of course. Though I might not answer.

Who are they?

Who are who?

The supera bounders.

She laughed.

Oh that's a great name for it. The supera bounders. That's exactly what they are.

And why do they want us to feel so temporary?

Again, a good way to put it.

And why are those machines they're using so rubbish? Don't we rate being bullied by something more technologically impressive?

She laughed out loud.

Well, Briar. It's been an unexpected pleasure spending this time with you. But now. Listen. In half a minute I'm going to stop stock still on the pavement. I want you to pass me by at a skipping rate like you don't know me, and then I want you to get yourself home and take great care, my new friend, of your young self.

I will if you will take great care of yours, I said.

My young self? she said.

Yes, her too, I said.

Aren't you a charmer. No worries about me, I'm a natural caretaker, she said. You be one too, now.

Do my best, I said.

Good. Right. When I say the word *now*, skip forward ahead of me. Okay?

Okay.

We'd turned a corner and a corner, were both now on the part of the street with the corrugated iron sheets that blocked the end of the street my sister and I were living in.

Now, she said.

I started to skip along the pavement.

She stopped, pretended to be a breathless old person.

A few seconds past her I sensed her gone. Though there was actually nowhere she *could* go – unless she'd doubled back on herself and round the corner very fast – because there was just this street, and the slabs of iron fence at the dead end of it.

But when I got to our house a few seconds later and turned my head there was no sign of her or anyone anywhere behind me.

Why are they trying to render us so temporary? was something I'd heard our mother saying to Leif one night back in our old life.

I was meant to be in bed asleep. I was lying flat on the floor of the upstairs landing. I liked Leif, he was the nicest one so far, I didn't want Leif to be over, and earlier they'd had an argument, I'd heard them, they almost never argued like that, like something jagged was happening. They usually argued more like overexcited small dogs playing a game that's got too hectic.

Now they were in bed and talking in a murmur and I wanted to be sure that it wasn't still an argument.

– group of people, Leif was saying, decides to [   ] another group of people it's usually to show off their power to themselves via the people they've designated as [ ]. And if [ ] can be made to feel, as you put it, temporary –

(so maybe *render us* meant something to do with making you feel something, I thought)

– Oh, I see. Then it's going to be about their own status as immortals, our mother said. Because nobody alive wants to believe, or actually can believe, psychologically, that they're temporary. Though we all are. Everybody is. There's no them or us when it comes to *that*.

[ ] a culture [ ] to demonstrate as more temporary than [ ]. Above all, people don't want to feel mortal, so [ ], Leif said.

Here endeth the lesson, our mother said. Are you always so bloody right?

[ ], he said.

Then there was the sound of them both happy, or happier, so he will have said something like *no not always only eleven times out of ten* which will have made her poke his side and laugh.

Relief, re Leif.

I'd rolled over, stood up, crept to my door and gone from there to the bathroom door, switched the bathroom light on in case they'd heard me up, run a tap, switched the light off again and got back into bed.

Next day I'd filched the laptop out of its hiding place and looked up the word render.

To melt down. To extract by melting. To convert

into industrial fats, oil or fertilizer. To give up or yield. To give in return or retribution. To cause to be or become. To make something or someone be in a particular altered state. To reproduce by artistic or verbal means. To apply a coat of plaster or cement directly to something. A return due from a feudal tenant to his lord.

It was always exciting to me the number of things a single word could mean.

I looked up to render temporary too, and discovered that rendering made walls more breathable and also that temporary render wasn't at all a good thing for a building or any surface and was likely to crack sooner rather than later.

The house hadn't burnt down with my sister locked in it. But maybe the only reason it hadn't was that my sister wasn't actually in the house to burn it down. Both front and back doors were still locked but the kitchen window was pushed open as high as it would go. There was a heap of green stuff and a lot of wilting little yellow flowers on the floorboards beneath it. It was like someone had come and dumped a lot of garden waste through the window.

She was strolling and bending, strolling and bending in the middle of the horse field, the horses unbothered, nose-to-grass as if she wasn't there. They all lifted their heads and turned to look at me crossing the field though, and when she saw them do that she looked round too and saw me.

Oh hi, she said.

She had a lot of pulled-up buttercups in her hand and was piling them into the open rucksack in her other hand.

You can help, she said.

Feed these to the horses?

No! she said.

Buttercups were bad for horses. Usually horses just don't eat them anyway, she told me, because they think they taste horrible. But she'd decided to pull up all the ones in this field in case they ate them by mistake.

How do you know they're bad for them? I said. This morning you were going to feed them tinned meatballs.

Colon told me, she said.

A boy called Colon had come and talked to her at the fence and told her his father owned this field.

He asked me a lot of questions, she said.

What kind of questions?

The usual boring kind, she said pulling some more up and heading for the next yellow specks. Then he told me that buttercups are bad for horses and blister their mouths if they eat them when they're still in the ground or not totally dried out, but that these horses are avatar horses so it doesn't matter if they eat them.

Did you just say avatar? I said.

Abba-tor, she said.

Abattoir? I said.

Uh huh. And I was watching the horses, she said, and they do generally just eat round them, like run their noses over the buttercups then leave them. But I thought that since I was here I'd remove them in case he got it wrong and the kind of horse that they are doesn't make any difference to whether eating buttercups blisters their mouths.

You know what an abattoir is, I said.

Uh huh. It's a kind of horse.

I looked all round the edges of the field but I couldn't see anyone.

How old is he, this person? Where does he live?

I don't know. Same as you? He was the one asking the questions, not me.

Did he have his father with him? Did his father ask you anything?

No! It was just him. It's okay. I told him we're visiting here staying with our aunt. I didn't tell him where. I didn't tell him anything. I'm not stupid.

Yeah but you're still stupid enough not to know what an abattoir is, I nearly said,

but I didn't.

Instead I agreed to do a run round the field looking for any pulled-up buttercups she'd dropped by mistake, then I followed her up and down it picking my way between the piles of horseshit, the smell of which I was beginning to quite like, holding the rucksack open so she could put the flowers straight in as she picked them. When it was full I carried the rucksack back to the house and emptied it where she'd dumped the others,

because, she said, I didn't want anyone thinking I was a vandal leaving piles of flowers I'd pulled up anywhere I shouldn't.

The horses ate the grass round us unperturbed.

We did the field till we were hungry ourselves. When we were, we went back and opened a tin of meatballs and shared them, after which we opened one of the tins of rice.

The empty house had the floor of one of its rooms strewn with flowers and a smell of earth and greenness all through its downstairs all night. Each morning for the next few days I scraped them up together, carried them into the garden and left them on the paving in the corner where they dried away to something nearly nothing and blew nothingly around in the paved yard for the rest of our time in that house.

So I've spent the last five years of my life not letting myself think any of this.

Occasionally though, over this time, a sharp-edged piece of it surfaced in me anyway, like a pottery fragment of something that was once a plate or a cup, an ordinary household thing, will if you're digging in the ground, and you see it, pick it up, wipe the earth off it and turn it over in your hand.

Rubbish? or keepsake? the thought of my sister shaking me awake in an empty house to come with her and help check for and clear a field of any flowers we'd missed, any flowers newly opening overnight, that might be harmful to horses, horses she didn't yet know were only there to be butchered, so that those horses wouldn't eat them by mistake and do damage to their soft mouths.

What does whistleblower mean?

Oh, sweet heart, our mother said.

She was in the doorway of the front room of the place we'd come to live in because we'd had to move. I was very small and standing in the front room where the damp smell which we were getting used to was. My sister was upstairs asleep. She'd stopped being the size that mostly just cries and was now more like a child than a baby but it was still good when she was asleep and it was just me and our mother, who crossed the room now and gave me a tight hug, which I resisted at first, then gave in to.

She sat me down on the couch next to the dog we called Rogie and she said,

stay here. I'll be back in a minute.

The dog was sleeping. He opened one eye, looked

to see who'd sat beside him, beat his tail on the cushion once, shut his eye again. His doghair was coarse at the same time as soft, warm against me. I looked at a paw, its long toes and claws, the leather of its underside black then in one place bright pink. I thought the paw looked like the foot of a gryphon; right then I was reading one of our mother's books about medieval people and it was full of pictures I couldn't stop looking at. One was a picture of a person being pulled apart by being tied to two horses which were both whipped to make them go in opposite directions. One was of a row of people standing in a line and each person was next to a skeleton; one of the people was pointedly ignoring their skeleton, another was looking scared to be standing next to their skeleton, another was conversing with their skeleton.

I checked the dog's nose was wet. If a dog's got a wet nose, that means he's well.

It was wet.

Our mother came back from the kitchen with a mug of hot chocolate. She'd made it with milk, not water, the way she only did when something important was happening.

She sat down on the other side of me.

A whistleblower means someone who tells the truth about something when other people don't want anybody to tell the truth about it.

?

You ask all the difficult questions, Bri. I shouldn't be surprised! You take after me. Okay. Well. Not long after you were born, as you know, I was working for the people who run the weedkiller conglomerate. Working there meant we had a bit more money, and I was putting money aside because I knew we'd need it, your sister was going be born soon, she was already on her way.

?

No. Thank goodness. They have chemists and lab people who do that. No, I was in charge of publicity copy. That's a kind of writing that people read and find persuasive enough to believe they really need to buy the product you're selling.

?

A product is, uh, products are the things they made and sold. A weedkiller conglomerate's product is weedkiller. So I was pregnant with your sister, you know what pregnant is, and I'd drop you off at the company's childcare unit every morning, that was a good unit, they even did some foundational teaching there for workers' kids. I mean. Childcare. Plum job, Bri. Then one day, I'd just left you there, I was on my way to the PR office, and one of the chemists, a lady who didn't work there any more, who'd worked there at the laboratory but left under a cloud, stopped me. She told me to go and get you and to take you home right away, and that if I had to come back there not to do it until after I'd had my baby, and then she said if I could get another job I was to get another job. And she told me a couple of things no one was meant to know. She said that the weedkiller conglomerate was using a chemical in their products that didn't just poison weeds and grasses and flowers and insects, but was also unsafe for lots of other bigger living things. Including dogs, and birds, and cows, and the milk that came from them. And she said that it was also dangerous for people, especially small children. Especially children who aren't born yet.

?

What? Ah. No. Under a cloud means they were suspicious of the lady. There was no actual cloud. But then this lady also told me a really important secret. She told me about their most popular product, the weedkiller they sold the most of. She knew my job was to persuade people how kind and gentle this weedkiller was and above all how good it was for the environment. How it could safely be used everywhere. What she told me was that this product had the exact same chemical formula as the conglomerate's most virulent product.

?

Strong in the wrong way. Strong enough to do damage, or to harm things, or harm us.

?

Yes, very like a monster. An invisible one. A really

dangerous one. And when I started quietly asking people difficult questions and finding things out for myself too I found out the lady was telling the truth, and while I was still finding this out I got a letter from the personnel department at Kindweed telling me I was being sacked and they were taking me to court.

?

Because the truth meant they'd have to change what they were doing, and they didn't want to. Because changing what they were doing meant they wouldn't make so much money. And the company not making so much money meant that a lot of people might lose their jobs.

?

Oh. I see. Ha. No. There isn't an actual whistle either. I wish there was, that'd be more fun. It's just what it's called, maybe because a whistle makes a loud noise? one that lots of people can hear above the usual noise, loud enough to make people listen? Like a referee in a football match blows a whistle when someone breaks the rules. Or to tell people the game's over.

?

Because a lot of people where we used to live rely on the place that makes it for their livelihoods. Their jobs. Their salaries. So they can pay for their houses, and eat enough, and feed their children.

?

Well, people like to think they can control nature. They think they can make where they live look better if they do. And sometimes weeds are virulent too, and insects are, they're more and more virulent now the weather is so hot, and the floodings. They can ruin essential crops and make people sick with a bite or a sting. Things sometimes need to be removed or controlled so people can grow things like food. But what I think now is this. For centuries we worked out how to do that in all weathers, without using chemical poisons. So it's not new work to us as a species. We'd just have to work harder at doing it right. And some of the insects that people don't like because they bite and sting are incredibly useful and even beautiful. And clever. Wasps, for instance, are clever pollinators. Bees. There used to be more than two hundred and seventy different types of bee when I was small. And those big hornets, I think they're beautiful as well as frightening. Like flying fuchsias, with their long legs hanging down.

?

Flowers, it's a kind of flower. Did you know you can eat fuchsias? And that they're even a help in healing some skin conditions?

?

Yes, and lots of flowers that people think are weeds. Well, bluebells, for one. And knapweed. Ragwort. Mayweed. Speedwell. Oysterplant.

Bindweed. Bugloss. Stonecrop. Campion. Willowherb. That's just off the top of my head. And willowherb is traditionally good for stomachs and breathing problems. I've a very nice book you can have, I'll go up and get it for you when we finish talking. Different forms of campion they thought might help stop bleeding, if you were bleeding inside, and be soothing for stings and warts and help people's inflamed kidneys, could be used to get some types of cloth really clean and in the old days it was even used to treat people who'd been bitten by snakes, and stonecrop's a help for blood pressure, and for wounds, and for people coughing. All the plants have uses, if we remember how to use them properly.

?

Oh, Bri. Because I needed the money. Because it seemed at the time like a very good way to make a living. It takes a lifetime, sometimes, to work out what anything you're doing's got to do with the real realities of living. Rather than what turns out to be the fake realities. But with any luck this won't be the story of your life, sweet heart.

?

Because you're already versatile, you're already all the possibilities. That's a godgiven gift, you know. You'll make things better, better than we did. You all will. You have to. Somebody has to.

?

Ah, now, well, Rose. Who knows? Rose is the wild one.

?

My life? Well. I tell you what, Bri. It's a puzzle all right and right now solving it is out of my hands.

?

Yes we will. That's what we'll do, sweet heart. We'll salve it.

Colon really was called Colon. I'd thought maybe my sister'd been punning on someone called Colin or she'd maybe misheard him saying his name.

He had the look, as I came towards him, of someone even more geeky than me.

Who're you? he said.

Brice, I said. Rose is my sister.

I'm Colon Kendrick, he said. Brice what?

I looked at him like I didn't understand.

Your surname, he said.

Why do you need to know my surname? I said.

Why don't you want to tell me your name? he said.

I told you. I'm Brice.

I told you my surname as well as my first name, he said.

I made up a surname.

Bush, I said.

Why are you in my father's field?

Is it a problem? I said.

Not as long as you don't open the gate.

My sister had come over to watch us speak. She lay down on her front on the ground and put her chin in her hands very like the happy children in the keyring.

I showed him my hands still full of the pulled fronds of buttercups.

We're collecting wildflowers, I said.

What for?

Our mother is a very important person who works at the weedkiller place at home where we live, which isn't anywhere near here. We're collecting samples from fields for her, my sister said.

Colon was now fiddling with a smartwatch on his wrist.

What's the place she works at called? he said.

Kindweed, my sister said.

What does she do there?

She's a whistlejacket.

What's that?

It's a very important job.

I gave my sister an impressed look. She smirked. Colon was holding his wrist out towards her.

Is your watch recording her? I said.

You mean my educator? he said.

Is it filming me? she said.

It automatically films everything, he said. Where's *your* educators?

He was looking at our arms.

I'm not picking up any data from yours with mine, he said. Why not?

We don't have them, my sister said.

Don't have them?

He looked shocked.

How do you get your education then? he said.

We choose to be educated by things bigger than something so small it can be worn on a human wrist, I said.

What other way is there? he said.

I gestured with both my arms to everything around us.

I don't get it, he said.

You know, I said. Being here. In person.

He looked thoughtful, then superior.

I suppose it's not everybody that can afford an educator, he said.

Then he told us some of the things his educator could do other than just educate. Heart rate, bloods, steps, nutritional breakdown of what you're eating, internet everything, camera, phone. Transform voice to text. Instantaneous translation but only forty languages (next model up more expensive does one hundred and thirty). Stream anything streamable. Tell the time.

He was still holding it pointing towards my sister.

Has no one told you yet that anodyne is the new digital? she said.

She was always mixing up the words anodyne and analogue. Sometimes I thought she did it on purpose.

Colon looked at her with his blank face.

Brice here says your name is Rose so if you both have the same surname you're called Rose Bush. Why did you tell me yesterday your name was Taylor Swift?

I didn't, my sister said. I told you my name was Taylor Smith.

I burst out laughing. My sister looked pleased.

Either way you were lying, he said.

I can't believe you thought I was telling you the truth if you thought what I was saying was that my name was Taylor Swift! my sister said.

Colon blushed.

Why wouldn't I? he said.

I should have told him I was one of the Beatles, she said to me.

One of the what? he said.

We both stared at him.

Are you an alien from another time? my sister said.

I'm from now, he said. I belong. I don't know where or when you're from. I don't get half of what you're saying about who you are or aren't. Or why yesterday you were telling me a lie when you were telling me your name was whatever it was.

It wasn't a lie. It's who I was yesterday. I change my name whenever I feel like it, my sister said. Sometimes I change it fifteen times a day. A person can have as many names as they like.

Yes but what's your name as recorded in the national register of births and marriages and deaths and on your passport? Colon said.

Passports. Last time we'd seen our passports Leif was tucking them into an inside jacket pocket.

Why are you both exchanging looks with each other? Colon said.

Is your name really Colon? I said.

He spelled it. It really was.

Who called you that?

Everyone calls me it. My father. My brother.

Have you got a little brother called Semi? my sister said. Or are you named after an ancestor's intestines?

He looked bewildered.

Is your second name Ization? my sister said.

I laughed. I couldn't not. My sister looked pleased again. But I was suddenly filled with bad feeling, like he'd think I was laughing at him, that we were being patronizing or unpleasant to him.

It's Kendrick. Look, I just need to know the answers to these other questions, he said.

Okay, I said. Tell me what the questions are first.

No, he said. That's not how this is done.

You have to, I said.

Why? he said.

So I have time to think up the answers, I said.

Why would you need time to think up answers? That's a bit like you might lie when you answer the questions because you've had time to think up another answer instead of the true answer.

No, I said. It's considered, and mindful. It means my answers will be more grounded in properly contextualized thought.

In what? Colon said.

They'll be better answers, my sister said.

She gave me a look like she knew how to deal with Colon better than I did.

People round here usually just answer my questions one after the other when I ask them without knowing or needing to know what I'm going to ask first, Colon was saying.

Yes but we're not from round here, I said.

No, my sister said. We're visitors to here.

Do they do data differently where you're from? he said.

Where we're from the person asking the questions *always* lets you see or know the questions first, I said. It's a formality.

Weird. Is that why your sister refused to answer the questions yesterday?

I find it weird that you'd expect me to do it any other way, I said.

Me too, Colon, my sister said.

Colon pushed his glasses up his nose.

Anyway, what're you doing asking people stuff off a stuffy questionnaire in the middle of your Easter break? I said.

I don't just do this in the Easter holidays, he said. I do it all year round.

It's a very strange hobby, I said.

I'm a local DDCS, he said. I'm the youngest local DDCS, locally I mean.

He put his hand in his back pocket and pulled out a lanyard with his photo on it and the letters DDC/S.

What does it stand for?

Don't you know? he said.

I don't think *you* know, I said.

I do so know!

If you tell me, I'll let you read me out all the questions you want to ask us, I said.

Designated Data Collector slash Strangers, he said. Obviously.

Who do you collect it for? Who do you give it to? my sister said. Is it for your father? Does he need that data on the farm?

Don't you two know anything? he said.

He turned to me.

You said you'd listen to me telling you my questions if I told you what it meant.

Did I? Well, if that's what I said, then okay. Tell me your list of questions.

Colon scrolled his watch.

Your date of birth your place of birth your ethnicity your gender your sexuality your religion your postcode your latest blood test figures your education level the education level of your parents the current and historic job status and income level of your parents the homeowner status of your parents the details about your parents regarding their employment or self employment. And any disabilities. What you think is the single most important issue facing us in this country today and anything else issue wise facing us today and whether you think immigration is a very big problem and whether you prefer dogs or cats and what you think is a general threat as concerns defence and foreign affairs and homegrown terrorism and which toothpaste you use and why. And whether you agree with most people that re-education is a good policy in the treatment of unverifiables. And whether you consider yourself a person who has ideas, and who you'll probably vote for if you're eligible to vote at the next three elections. And whether you think climate change is real and what your favourite colour is and whether you think homegrown environmental protest terrorists should be exiled along with illegal immigrants and do you prefer to shop online or offline. And which social media platforms do you use and what for and which platforms do you like most and least and which do you trust most and least. And depending on which product we're featuring, this week it's Patchay painkillers, there's a separate list of questions about them I'll ask when we get to them that also covers the full range of Requiescat health products. And finally. What your favourite number is and which number it's best to reach you at.

[Pause.]

And you have to answer truthfully, he said. Or they'll know.

Who'll know? my sister said.

He turned to look at her and shook his head in despair. She gave him an open glance back and I could see that she quite liked him and he quite liked her.

Colon, I said.

I said it not like I was saying his name but like I was thinking about his name.

What? he said.

I bet you get bullied a lot, I said.

A flush went up Colon's face from his neck and reached his forehead.

You are bullying me now by not answering my questions, he said.

No, this isn't bullying. And I'm going to rechristen you Colin. From now on, instead of that other name, to me you're Colin.

Why? he said.

Just to see what happens, I said.

You can be someone else! my sister said.

I'm already someone, he said. No person on earth can just 'be' someone else.

How much money do passports make if you steal them and sell them? my sister asked me.

Very good money, I said.

We were both sitting on the top bar of the fence, the horse field behind us, watching Colin's rounded shoulders going up the path towards some farm buildings. I was plaiting some of the just-pulled buttercups into the long strand of my hair next to my left eye and down past my shoulder. My sister was decorating my hair at the back of my neck with a weave of them too.

We should've asked him, I said. His watch could've told us how much.

Why do they? she said. Make a lot?

People who don't have them need them, I said, and can buy them if they can afford them.

Now we don't have them. Will we need them? Can we afford them?

We can tell anyone who needs to see one of ours to look us up on their system and we'll be there, I said. Anyway. They're safe. Leif has them. When he comes back we can ask him for them.

Do you think he's there yet?

I don't know.

Do you think he's seen her yet?

I shrugged.

Do you think maybe Leif's taken our passports on purpose and he's going to sell them for very good money?

No, I said.

Why?

I trust Leif.

Why? she said.

Because our mother trusts him.

Yeah but she trusted other people in the past and now they're not here either, are they? my sister said.

Leif is kind, I said. He's never hurt us and meant it.

That's true, she said.

When he carries you on his shoulders he always puts you down on the ground carefully afterwards.

He does, she said. But he left us on our own. We're underage.

Because he knew we wouldn't want to live with people we didn't know when he went to get her. So he went out of his way to sort something workable for *us*. He entrusted *us*. He trusts us to be here when they get back. If he wanted to just leave us he'd have just left us. At Tesco. Outside the old house. With the Upshaws. At one of the passport places. Wherever.

He's not our family, she said. That's what the people in the passport offices kept saying to us.

Yeah but that's okay, I said. Family can be more things than people say it is.

Yeah, I know, she said.

Also. He'll come back to get the money he gave us, I said. He told me he wants it back.

It isn't very much money, she said.

Then she said,

Bri. What actually is trust?

Eh, I said. It's. You know.

I don't, she said.

You trust me, yeah?

First tell me what it is then I'll tell you, she said.

I tried to think of a way to say it. I thought how that morning she'd gone ahead to get to the field and when I came through the hedge and across the path I'd been relieved there were still horses in the field for her to see at all. Then I'd seen the grey horse raise its head when it saw her coming towards the field. When it did it began to amble towards her. Some of the other horses had seen it do this, they'd all lifted their heads and watched her arrive, and a couple of them had followed the grey one for a while then stopped. When she climbed over the fence the grey horse had been waiting, had come and stood beside her and she'd reached up and patted its neck.

The horse, I said. The grey one.

Gliff, she said.

How do you mean cliff? I said.

Not cliff. G. Gee el eye eff eff.

What's that mean? I said.

It's the name I've given it.

What sort of a name's that?

Well, she said. Yesterday I was trying to talk to Colon about the horses while he was trying to get me to answer his questions, and I asked him their names and he told me he didn't know any of their names. Or even if they'd ever had names. When I said, not even that grey one? he said, oh the grey one, my father says be very careful round that horse, that's a very gliffy horse. So I tried calling it Gliffy in my head but that felt like making it smaller and made it sound like it was an iffy horse. So I took the y off and that felt more right, more like its name should.

An if horse. Not an iffy horse, I said.

Yep, she said.

What does it mean, the word?

I don't know, she said. That's why I like it.

Well. I was thinking about how you gave it grass to eat yesterday, I said.

Yeah, she said. So?

And then, did you give it more to eat when you came up to the field again from the house later yesterday?

No, she said. I didn't have anything to give it or any time to get it more of the longer grass because first Colon was there and was speaking a lot, and then after that I wanted to get the buttercups out as much as possible.

So it saw you in the distance today and it was pleased to see you, and not for any reason like food, it just knew it knew you, it knew you're not going to do anything horrible to it –

No way, she said.

– like it's pleased to see you.

Yeah, I like it, too, she said.

An agreement or understanding between you.

Okay, she said.

One that doesn't even need words.

Uh huh, she said.

So. That's trust, I said.

Oh. Okay. So. You think the agreement that doesn't need words between us and Leif means he took our passports by mistake or maybe for safe keeping and he *won't* sell them or lose them?

I mean yeah he might lose them, I said. Or they might get stolen. But anyway even if he did, even if he sold them, we're on the system. They've got our names and details and photos and passport numbers. Our mother would pay them some money and they'd just check their system and make us a new one.

And you still think Leif will come back? He's not coming back.

Don't say that, I said.

Is that not allowed words, then? she said.

Not going to happen, I said.

What do we need passports for? she said.

So we can travel to other countries and prove we're us, I said.

Yeah but a passport doesn't prove we're us, she said. We prove a passport's *it*. We just *are* us. We're us right now and we don't have any passports to prove we're us. Not having a passport doesn't mean we, what, *disappear*.

Now you're being stupid, I said. Anyway soon we won't even need passports. All we'll need is our eyes and our fingers for proof of who we are.

Is it so we belong to a system and then the system becomes the thing that can decide stuff about us? And what if someone goes through the system, she said, and they decide to mark round our names and what was it, details, or our photos and passport numbers, and any scan of our eyes and fingers, like with the red paint? We'd still be us. Wouldn't we? I mean I know there's no red paint thing happening *here*. And that maybe it's just what happened *there*. But we're still *us*. Yeah?

I thought of the building in town yesterday and the spill of red outside it. *It belongs to the people who've bought it*. Maybe the supera bounder people had bought our house too and we just didn't know it. I thought of Mr Upshaw at the front door and Leif and him standing examining the place where the red marking stopped, the place where the houses in the terrace became his house not ours. But then, why did the supera bounders also want our old rusting campervan?

So he can sell the passports if he wants, my sister was saying jumping down from the fence. Or lose them, whatever. Or come back, or not. I'll still be me.

She looked up at me. She looked very small and bright beneath me, her forehead sunlit.

Sometimes I think you're a very old and wise person disguised as you, I said.

Thanks, she said.

And sometimes, I said, I think you're one of the youngest greenest people I'll ever know.

I am all my me's, she said. I am complete.

She did a pirouette back up the fence, up and over it, and landed on her feet on the other side. She turned, waved over her shoulder at me then started towards the horses, which were mostly heads down eating over on the far side of the field.

The grey horse raised its head.

It was already walking towards her.

I was sitting on the front wall watching the people who walked up and down the street go past looking at their phones. They all did. Much as I envied every person who had one and who could call their own mother on it, or anyone else, and look up anything at all any time they liked, our mother was right.

They did nothing but look at their phones.

It made them stumble about.

I decided not to envy them.

In honour of our mother I would look properly at what was happening around me instead.

For instance, what was that big white sign tacked up across one of the corrugated iron panels?

I was about to go and see what it said when someone, a girl a bit older than me and the first person I'd seen rounding the corner not looking at a phone, came into the street, went right up to the fence, stepped into it and vanished.

But there was no door. The fencing was nothing but fencing.

I jumped off the wall.

CAUTION!
UNSAFE PREMISES
WARNING
Do Not Enter.
Area Closed for Public Safety Reasons.
Any unauthorized person
removing this sign
will be prosecuted.

I read it then I walked the length of the fencing and back again. It ran the whole breadth of our quite wide street from one side to the other, double height, as tall as the buildings on either side, taller in some places. I read the sign again. The sign was declaring it'd be a more punishable thing to do to remove *it* than to wander about in whatever unsafe thing or place was behind this fencing.

While I stood thinking about that a brown cat walked straight through the iron sheeting. It stopped, sat on the pavement not far from me and surveyed me and the street. Then it set off up the road and disappeared into a driveway on the opposite side of the road from our house.

It had come through a slim space between two overlapping sheets of the corrugated iron. The space was so slim it didn't look big enough for that cat, even. I pressed the underlayer sheet slightly and it gave, its bottom half bowed away from me to reveal itself as a false wall which met the front layer at the top and made a corrugated dark tent.

I slipped in between the layers sideways like the filling in a sandwich. The space was the width of a cat and only just the height of me. Dark one way, a bit of daylight the other way. To turn my head to see this I had to rub my nose and chin on one of the metal ridges.

Along through the two layers of fencing towards the light the inside layer gave into an opening. I had to flatten myself more and edge down lower than my own knees to get through the cut in the metal like a small hatch which someone had worked the edges of to make them blunt and folded so they wouldn't cut open a person or a creature going through.

I fell out into vast greenness.

In this green, in the light and the space, I got to my feet and rubbed at the rust on my face and clothes.

Wild grasses stretched away in all directions like this was some kind of park. There was a slight indentation of path in this grass that began at the hatch. It went down into an overgrown football field, to the side of which was a long rectangular building, once white, now peeling, with big windows upstairs and down all covered with chipboard.

It didn't look publicly unsafe from the outside. It looked sturdy. Maybe it was unsafe on the inside. Maybe whoever fenced it off and put the sign up was warning people that something in here was a cultural threat to the public. Cultural threats were everywhere according to the socialnet and socialweb. As if blocking it off with an iron fence five metres high wasn't enough of a sign. I could see as I crossed the grasses that the fencing stretched all the way round this place like a giant had outlined it with a pen made of rust, and that it must be backing up to people's gardens and the yards at the backs of small shops and blocking off bits of a lot more streets than just ours.

There were grand flat stone steps leading up to a double door. Above it in the stone of the building was the carving of a shield, weatherworn, with something that looked a bit like a blunted lion on one side and maybe what was once a unicorn on the other. Arched over them, over the shield:

SCHOOL of ST SACCOBANDA

1902

and inside the shield more words eaten by time:

facta sunt ipse verba

or maybe

pacta sunt ipse verba

or iacta. Or tacta. They sounded like words that had meanings but they weren't words I knew.

Can you read that? someone behind me said.

I can. What does it mean? I said.

It means you shouldn't be here and you'd better go back to where you came from fast, the girl said.

If that's what it says then it's telling the story of my life, I said.

The girl gave me a double take.

How did you get in here? she said.

Through the, you know.

I gestured behind me back to the fencing.

Catflap, I said.

She laughed. She was a few years older than me, sixteen maybe.

You look like you're wearing the costume of someone in an apocalyptic sci fi film about people who live underground after a disaster, I said.

You don't look so haute couture yourself, she said. You really need a wash.

Why does it say it's publicly unsafe in here? I said.

Oh yeah, the signs, she said. They're there to let you know how dangerous it is in here.

What is it? Is it a school?

Do you not know the old saying about what happens to curious cats?

I'm not scared, I said. I'm not scared of anything.

More fool you, she said.

She gave me quite a hard push in the collarbone.

Go on, you little litter-runt. You can't be in here.

How do I get out? I said.

Same way you came in, she said. And if I catch you in here again I'll uh tell the authorities I saw you taking their signs down. So don't come in again. You'll fucking regret it if you do, there's some very big dogs in here.

She waited, watched me cross the playing field grass. Halfway over I turned and waved goodbye.

Pushing your luck, pussycat, she shouted.

It still looked like there was almost no water in the bath though there were already five kettlefuls in it. I was deciding which pieces of my clothing to wash and hoping it would work to wash clothes and myself without any soap. Me first, then the item of clothing. The only problematic day would be the day I had to wash and dry my jeans. Everything else could be improvised. But with any luck we'd be gone to, to where? to whatever home we'd be living in, with our mother and Leif, well before that day happened.

So I was in the bathroom of that empty house when my sister came back, came upstairs, sat on the floor of it and told me, staring straight at me, that she now knew what abattoir meant.

Who had told her? Colon's elder brother Posho. Posho had told her about the bolt gun, the knives, the skinning, the butchering, the rendering, the glue, the meat for dogs and the meat falsely sold to people as beef. Posho had explained to her that there were abattoirs for people too though they didn't always begin by slaughtering people straight off like with animals. Instead they retrained them, if their education hadn't been the right kind or done to the right level, and then gave them jobs to do. Posho knew because he was working as a handyman for one of the new Adult Retraining Centres. Or arks, as in Noah. The people in them weren't really people. They were animals. They also re-educated kids, according to Posho. The kids were held in equivalent Child Retraining Centres, or circuses. The kids in them weren't really kids. They were animals. You were lucky though if you weren't yet an adult because adults got majorly foul jobs mostly to do with human shit and the waste products of the industrial and power places and if they refused to do these jobs then they were gone from whichever ark next day and nobody saw them again ever, or knew where they got taken. Kids, though, were given very specific jobs more suited to the sizes of their hands, they could get given, say, a crate of old dental floss plastic containers from which they'd have to unpick the metal slicer from the plastic cartridge and put the cartridge in one recycle tray and the slicer in another. The older ones, like her age, he said, had to get the metals out of old batteries. There was a big workforce churnover on this job because they had to do it with no gloves.

My sister told Posho he was a wind-up merchant.

Posho told my sister she'd find out soon enough and that she was a silly little cunt and would get what was coming to her and what came to all silly little fishy smelling cunts who should be in the kitchen and not out in the outside world, and that she'd no idea yet and the day would come when someone would pin her down and choke it all out of her and that'd be the day she'd be taught what she deserved and what all girls wanted in a man's world and that he hoped he'd be there to see it if it wasn't him actually doing it with his own hands and his own big dick.

Then Colon interrupted very fast so my sister wouldn't get a chance to say anything in reply to Posho and started telling her, as if Posho wasn't there, that their mother up at the farm had had some weedkiller spray bottles delivered and the label came off one of the bottles and it had a note written on the inside of it saying it was from someone whose job was to screw the sprayheads on to bottles that the factory machine had mis-screwed, and it said it was from an eleven year old who was getting sick from breathing weedkiller and wanted someone to help them. Which must have been a lie, his mother'd said, because the weedkiller said on the other side of the label that it was the bio-pure kind and that there was nothing poisonous to humans in it. Which is why she'd bought it.

You said your mother worked in a weedkiller company, Colon said, so she can tell you what the truth is and then you can tell me and I can tell my mother.

My sister had asked what their mother had done about the note she found. Colon said she'd put it in the pigs' feed with all the other bits of paper and cardboard and plastic that get recycled into the pigfood.

Posho got bored because nobody was listening to him and he left and though Posho was heading back over to the farm Colon stayed at the field hopping from foot to foot like there was something urgent, and as soon as Posho was out of earshot Colon'd shown her he wasn't wearing his educator by pulling up his sleeves and showing her his bare wrists and he'd said I shouldn't be telling you this but you two are coming up on facial as possible UVs, and when she said did that mean ultraviolets he'd looked at her like she was a person walking a tightrope with no net. He'd said did she never read the news on any of her devices. She'd rolled her eyes, told him we didn't have any vices and asked him when the horses would get taken and Colon told her the livestock markets were every Friday.

Then my sister, looking at me as if appraising me standing next to the bath still holding the steaming kettle I hadn't emptied into it yet, said,

what day is it today?

Every classic old horse story I've ever chanced upon in this brave new unlibraried world deals with the bloodiness of humanity to other creatures as well as each other and more often than not ends in dutiful sadness as if the story, not totally broken, is at least broken in.

Fast forward a few days. It was an extremely hot day. It was still April. The week before it had been so cold that we'd sometimes needed buttoned-up duffelcoats on inside the house. This week the temperatures veered between forty and forty five degrees.

So we were being wise and keeping cool by standing in the shady assembly hall at the centre of what was once St Saccobanda Sixth Form College.

We were looking up at a picture, black and white and grey and huge, hanging on the wall high above the hall's stage. Beneath it generations of young people would have said their prayers, done their exams, sung their school songs.

The picture was of a white horse in front of a cave. The horse was reversing so fast away from something frightful it'd seen that its mane and tail were flowing unnaturally forward, almost horizontal, like a freak wind was blowing them. Beyond it, emerging from the dark, a lion. The lion was turning towards – the horse? Us? It seemed to be looking past both the horse and us below it looking up at it.

The horse was lightning white, all electricity. The lion was calm, dark, massive-pawed, dripping surreptitiousness. The horse, dismayed. The lion, shifty. Below the horse's hooves, scattered outside the stony entrance to the dark shape of the cave, were rocks, plants, flowers. Some of the plant leaves looked like amputated human tongues.

We were standing with Ulyana Yusef, one of the people who lived in this building.

She was, I know now, I didn't know then, already a renowned philosopher and art historian, one who'd not long before been made stateless. Then I knew her, and will always remember her, as what she was to us, a homeless person being kind to two very young homeless people.

We were standing one on either side of her and

she was telling us about the English artist famous for painting and drawing beautiful horses.

He did many other pictures all very like this one too, she said, of a horse in a state of shock and fear when it sees a lion, and of a horse literally in the process of being attacked and mauled to death by a lion.

Stubbs? Rose said. Was that really his name?

Ulyana nodded.

These pictures became famous as versions of the sublime, she said.

More like the opposite of sublime, my sister said.

Not sublime the adjective, Ulyana said. Sublime the noun.

But sublime means like best thing ever, my sister said.

When you add a the, Ulyana said, to turn sublime into the sublime, it means you are seeing or experiencing something so shockingly awe-inspiring that your thoughts are raised to a spiritual plane of understanding, closer to an understanding of God or the gods.

My sister shook her head.

I don't get it, she said.

About what's beyond being human, Ulyana said. About how to experience something that elevates you, fills you with wonder because it's amazing and terrifying and is both of these things at the same time. Stubbs borrowed the idea from a very famous

Roman statue of a little horse that's collapsing under a massive lion. The lion in this statue is right up over the little horse's back, biting and clawing into its side. It's meant to be an allegory for accepting your own defeat as inevitable, and accepting it gracefully. Though really it's an allegory for how you're meant to give in to the might of empire, Mamma Roma the lion. And so on. I saw it once, it's a very beautiful, very terrible statue, both. And somewhere I read that the Romans liked to stand people next to that statue to announce to them that they were being condemned to death. To help them accept their fate. Like saying, look, it happens to the best of horse. And I can also tell you exactly how Stubbs got the look of fear that you can see in this picture into all the pictures he made of horses with lions threatening them.

How? my sister said.

He did it by standing a very nervous thoroughbred in a yard, a very beautiful horse like this one, and tethering it tightly to a ring in the wall so it couldn't move very much. Then he paid a stable boy to sweep the yard near the horse and to do it with a brush that had a very wide head and a very long handle, to sweep closer and closer to the horse's feet, increasingly aggressively, until the horse was wild with fear and pulling like mad against the tether. At which point he sketched it.

What a total outright cheat, my sister said.

Ah, but you can't cheat the sublime, Ulyana said.

Yeah well, there must be other sublimes, my sister said.

Oh, there are, Ulyana said. Astonishing beautiful visions of nature so awe-inspiring that they look supernatural. A blood red sun in a storm. Someone standing on a rock at the top of a mountain watching clouds roar beneath him like a wild sea. Volcanoes spilling their deep red lava into darkness. But they're always dark, these images, and always about both dark and light, and they are always unsettling. Because if you aren't unsettled, then there'll be no sublime.

Well, I want a new sublime, my sister said. A different sublime.

Do you, now? Ulyana said.

I'll be both sublime and *the* sublime, my sister said.

Will you, now? Ulyana said.

I'll be the horse that pulls that ring right out of that wall and tosses it about in the air on its tether, I'll be the horse chasing the stable boy to bite him in the back with my big horse teeth for scaring me because someone told him to or paid him to. And then I'm off after that painter, to shove his easel over and his water jar and crush his paints and his pencils underhoof and kick him all the way out of that yard for scaring me for such stupid reasons with a stupid brush, my sister said.

Ulyana put one arm round my sister and the other arm round me.

Meanwhile, what was I doing?

I was standing silent as if my own tongue had been cut loose from its root and fallen, a too-thick leaf on the floor of my mouth.

I'll stub Stubbs out, my sister was saying.

I don't think any of us gets to tell the sublime what to do, Rose, she said.

Pff, my sister said.

Brave new world:

then there's this, which in the end – or maybe the beginning – might be called a sister moment to the one above. It's a moment that's proved to be my own sublime.

Fast forward five years to the person I'm meant to be right now.

As usual I get sent someone reprimanded for poor line behaviour at the Packing Belt in the Delivery Level.

She stands in my office in front of my desk. She looks for a moment familiar, does she? No, I look again and I'm pretty sure I don't know her after all.

According to the initial report she's been missing codematches on items and packing things in too messy a fashion. There's also the matter of a dropped and smashed jar of preserved onions on the Packing Belt floor.

I look at her hands. One is a blunt stub.

The other is deformed too, though not as badly, with just a deep burn scar right the way across it and up past the wrist.

Before I get a chance to say anything she says,

fuck me, you are the image of your sister.

Nobody these days knows I had a sister. It's fallen off any data connected to me unless you go really far back, pre-digital, and find something as yet un-erased, which, when I do, I am careful to delete; I've paid a lot of my (very good) salary to people to learn how to delete, and she now exists nowhere on any system to which I have access – and I have access to ninety nine per cent of them.

You're mistaken, I say. I don't have a sister.

The image, she says again.

She is staring at me.

You're not here to smalltalk, I say.

Silence.

Then I say,

I'm instructing you to meet me down at the Packing Belt to demonstrate visually to me exactly what the problem is so I can deal fully and fairly with the report I've been asked to make on your progress.

I send her down the stairs on foot. I go down in the lift as per. Lift demarcation is one of the perks.

People will literally fistfight for a position that grants lift demarcation.

When I get down to the Delivery Level I can see no sign on the floor of a smashed jar. Someone's already dealt with that. Good. I don't have to. The complications of dealing with breakage are legion.

I wait at the foot of the stairs and when she arrives I point at the space next to the open mouth of the dispatcher.

No worker ever stands here. It's forbidden because here the Belt engine makes an infernal level of noise that interferes with sound monitoring. But it's a natural enough move; the Belt elsewhere is lined with codematchers bent over it picking out the items and scanning and packing them.

The person is still staring. She bends towards me and says too near my ear,

you're so like her that for a second I thought you were her.

I act like she's said nothing. I bend towards the Belt. I put my hand in front of my mouth. I make it look like an I'm-thinking gesture. She sees me do it and she raises her stump, partly to hide her mouth, partly as if showing it to me. It's now so close to me that I can see the scar skin.

Long time ago, she says. I was still a kid. We were all off our heads, it was a time when I was taking whatever I could get whenever I could get it, anything, we all were. Except her, she never took anything. We were holed up in the same cave, seven of us, we were there for quite a few weeks. I have to tell you. One of the people I most loved that I ever met. When someone's spirit never gutters.

All through her saying this I am thinking words like scam and entrapment. I make my face blank, pretend to look at the mechanism in front of me like an expert looking for faults in it. Meanwhile my heart is racketing inside my ribs so loud that it sounds inside me louder than the Packing Belt mechanism and I am full of fury at some stranger endangering me with her casual intimacy about a sister nobody knows I have. Worse – some stranger claiming to know more about my sister than I know. Whatever she's saying, whatever she's about to say, whether it's truth or lies, it's fixing my sister in a place and a time, and I resent this, and now this stranger is saying,

told me that if I ever met someone who looked really like her that I was to say hello from her and remind them about –

and then she says the word.

Gliff.

The word unbalances me so much I nearly fall forward into the fast flow of pickled vegetables rolling through on the Belt.

She's still speaking:

all took stuff. We had to, we all had body shit and we loved Patchay, best of the painkillers, just zapped it, blanked it out, blanked us out too. We all took it except her and she had this word for us, for it. She'd sit against the wall and watch out for us while we were on it, and she'd always say what we were was gliffed. We reckoned she was riffing on the old word spliff. So we all started calling it, whatever we took after that, gliff. And she told me, she told us all, that if we ever met you you'd help us, because you always help a fellow, especially if they're travelling.

You have to stop speaking, I say. Do you understand? There is no speaking on the Packing Belt floor.

Brave new wo ld:

surname?

Falcon.

Christian name?

I don't have one of those.

I sigh as if exasperated, as the cameras in my office will expect of me.

First name?

Ayesha.

Age?

I just turned seventeen.

That makes this person one year younger than me and roughly twelve years old when the injuries happened. Dear God. The back of my neck comes out in a cold sweat. But I do as I'm meant to, I read the screen text that blinks up under her name, first entry early in the first tranche of UV listings from when they widened UV to include ethnicity/creed/disability.

Date and place of birth? I say. Date and place of CRC entry? Date and extent of claimed damage? Self inflicted?

She shakes her head. Battery injuries, she says. Verified, on record.

Date of CRC Completion?

I never completed. I uh, left, before completion, she says.

Then she smiles and looks up at me from under her fringe.

They caught me. Obviously. But not for a while.

I don't smile. I nod with my eyes to the positions of the cameras in the room corners. She looks glancingly herself at the one above my head and says,

I've seen the error of my ways, obviously. Completely, since then, been through thorough readjustment, it should detail that on my records. Can you put it in, please, if it's not on there?

Your records can't be altered by me, I say. You'd have to go through the proper process.

I look at the screen.

It says here you've been given the position to which you were assigned because you've been rated physically able to perform it, I say. Why have you performed it poorly today?

Some days I guess I'm just less able than others, she says.

Because it's your first offence on this placement there's no immediate action to be taken against you. This meeting and this report are a warning. You'll be fined on a second offence. A third offence results in a salary moratorium. In other words you'll then be working for nothing until deemed fit for salary again. A fourth offence results in a period of readjustment in whichever ARC to which you'll be allocated.

Okay, she says. I understand. Thank you Mr, uh.

I fill in the report release, send it, print out a copy and sign and stamp it. I file the one on the screen. I nod into the screen camera then I glance at the camera at the back of the room and the front of the room and nod at them too, as if clearing her release.

I hand her the printed copy.

You'll need this to pass back through security, I say. Losing it or dropping it will be counted as a second offence.

She takes it in her less damaged hand.

Oh. And. Given the nature of your report you're entitled to one of these.

I open the locked drawer, take out the box, unlock it. She tucks her release form under her damaged arm and I place the painkiller in her hand. It's a double.

This is because the doubles are big enough to write on.

I am hoping her eyesight is still good enough.

She looks down at it, nods a thanks. I don't know whether this means she's read what's on it or not. She doesn't register surprise or collusion in any way.

Don't make a habit of this, I say. It's your responsibility to medicate yourself, not the company's. Any pain or discomfort you have on our time that results in poor work performance after today will still register as a second offence and you'll be liable for an immediate fine. Do you need a glass of water?

Yes. Half a glass would be great, thank you, she says.

I pour her a glass of water and she puts the painkiller in her mouth.

My sister and I were both still sitting in the bathroom of the empty house, our backs against the bath, the hardly any water in it long gone cold.

If anyone threatens you again like that you have to tell me. And I'll kill them, I said.

Nah, she said. You won't. That's the kind of thing you think you're supposed to say. And Posho was saying the kind of thing he thought he was supposed to say too. Loads of them say that stuff about girls, the ones that are most threatened by girls do. Some of the boys and men think it makes them more superior to say that stuff. They hate to think something outside them can see them and maybe judge them. It's not just men or boys, a lot of people are threatened by knowing that people who they think aren't anything like them exist. Yeah, though some of them *do* actually want to do that stuff to the people they threaten, and some of them do actually do it. Anyway if anyone did it to me, I'm telling you. I'd kill them myself.

Arks. Circuses, I said.

What if it's true? she said.

I shook my head.

How do you salve that? she said. What do we do?

What we can, I said.

I tried to sound like our mother.

And market day, she said. What we going to do about that?

If we're still living here tomorrow and they're not back from Alana's to get us yet we'll do, I don't know what. Something.

They're not coming back, she said.

I said, instead, to ward off this thought,

did you know that horses have been in the room at every important legal proceeding in a law court in this country since the 1600s?

Is this a joke? she said.

It's the only thing I know about horses, I said.

I told her how after finding out our mother had been up in court when we were small I'd filched the laptop one day and looked up stuff about courtrooms online, and that I'd read there that judges' and lawyers' wigs had traditionally been made and still more often than not were made of horsehair.

No! she said.

Maybe it's why there's the little ponytail at the back of some wigs, I said. It means horses have been a little bit present at every important thing, just or unjust, carried out in a courtroom in this country since the seventeenth century.

Wow, she said. So many bits of dead gone horse on so many powerful people's heads, yeah? Imagine real horses in there. Imagine them there at the trial, and our mother in the, what's it called, the place people have to stand?

Dock, I said.

We should all be being judged and decided about by horses, she said.

Then she said,

imagine if a dock in a court was made of dock, I mean dock *leaves*.

Then,

oh, and what's rendering? I mean I know what skinning is. I know what butchering is.

To render is to do with making people feel something. It's also something to do with tenants and lords, I said. Or it can also mean like applying a coat or layer of plaster or cement.

To a horse? she said.

Then it can also mean to melt something.

Melt a horse? she said.

And to make something be in an altered state, I said. Also, to give something up.

Yeah, well, getting skinned and butchered would make a horse give up all right, she said.

I got the roll of cash out of my pocket.

Would that buy the grey horse? I said.

Gliff, she said. I don't know. I don't know how much horses cost.

I gave it to her. She looked at it in her hand. Then she looked at me.

What if we need it for something else? she said.

We need it for this, I said.

What if we run out of food? she said.

She told me she wouldn't be eating meatballs any more since they were definitely cheap meat and therefore might also contain horse.

It may not be anywhere near enough, I said. Do it tomorrow. Don't deal with Posho, he'll just take it. Deal with Colin. Don't get the money out anywhere near his educator, and when you do, don't say anything. Just hold the money so he can glimpse it, glance at your horse, look back at the money and look at him again and see what he says. Then if he freaks or doesn't know what you mean you can pretend you were just, you know, showing him some money you earned for something, and that it's nothing to do with the horses, you were just looking over towards them because you heard something, a bird or something, behind you.

She nodded.

There are six other horses, she said.

I shook my head.

We have to, she said.

Okay. We'll uh.

I thought about it.

We'll let them out. At night. Tomorrow night.

We will, she said.

We'll open the gate so if they want to go they can. We'll need something to cut the chain with, I said.

She peeled a note, then another note, off the roll in her hands and gave them to me. I put them in my pocket.

We sat for a while saying nothing in the bathroom.

Don't do that, I said. (She was biting a nail.)

Sorry, she said.

Then, a little later, she said,

heart rendering. Like covering your heart in concrete at the same time as melting it and giving it up.

Oh. That's good, I said.

She got up and went through. When she came back she was carrying the bit of the doll that she'd taken from home.

Can I wash this? In that water you put in there? she said.

Why not? I said.

She did.

Then she sat back down beside me and shook the water out of the holes for its limbs on to the floor. She rubbed the bits of doll on her sleeve to get them dry.

Scarlet Town's very own Briar. I hoped I'd run into you again one day.

From nowhere she was standing next to me in her long black coat. I'd been outside the station now three mornings one after the other making sure I was standing exactly where I'd first seen her challenging the man with the supera bounder machine.

On the first day I'd watched the hoarding going up round the building that man had been trying to supera bound. The painted line round it was vibrant red, the hoarding placed just inside it so it was still visible. On the second day the machines had arrived, bulldozer after bulldozer and a truck with a great claw arm on the back of it, and the hoarding had opened, the machines had rolled in and the hoarding had closed again with just the claw showing above the roof of the building. Today where the building had been was nothing but air, the hoarding had been shunted to one side to display the gap, a raked platform with large spotlights on either side of it had been erected in front of the empty space and a lineup of men and women in suits was standing in the space next to one of the bulldozers, shaking hands with each other, smiling, making speeches I couldn't hear and being filmed by a wall of people arranged at different levels on the raked platform who were all holding what my sister would call their vices high like torches of liberty.

How's you? Sharp pointed as ever? she said not looking at me.

I am actually waiting here specifically to see you, I said.

Did you know you can talk to someone without moving your lips very much? she said. Try it the next time you say something to me.

What are those people over there doing? I said.

That's right. That's very good. Well done. What they're doing over there is photo-op shots of themselves at a celebratory demolition.

It was such a nice old building, I said.

You're right. It was both old and nice. They've been looking for an excuse to knock it down for years. So they can build another building there instead. Prime real estate position. There's not much you can use an old theatre for, except, you know, plays, concerts, films, things people love to see or to listen to together, old fashioned things like that, communal entertainment, endless imagination. This one's been shut to the public now for two years.

Is that because everybody has devices now instead? I said.

When it was open, right up to the end of it being open to the public, there weren't many days it wasn't completely sold out, whatever was showing. It's the first thing people wanted to do after the lockdown years. People like going to the theatre with each other. Well, they did. Though it's true that when they came back it was rowdier and more, shall we say, audience participatory than anyone was used to, though I imagine that made it quite like the old music hall years in there, everybody yelling and joining in and singing along and throwing things at the stage. Did you ever go to a theatre?

No, I said. What did people throw?

Oh, everything. Flowers. Stones. Bottles. Empty Coke cans. Full Coke cans, sometimes. Human excrement. Depended what was showing. Depended if they agreed with what they were seeing or not. And a lot of people who went to things did prefer, you're right, just looking at their devices all the time even in a theatre they'd paid their money to come and watch something in.

So is that why they supera boundered it?

Since it shut its doors some people who had nowhere to live were using it to live in over the winters. And last week there was the big nationwide drive to remove unverifiables. Much fanfare. They went in and round-upped everyone, took them off to God knows. Then they red-marked the building. Or they tried to. Till you spannered the works, my friend.

Till I what? I said.

Old figure of speech from back when people who worked with machines carried spanners, she said. In any case our spannering didn't disrupt them for long. There was red all round it next morning.

What's unverifiables?

Unverifiables are people.

Oh.

She told me more about unverifiables but I wasn't really listening, I was imagining our neighbours Mr and Mrs Upshaw standing in front of a space of air and flattened rubble next to their house right where our living room had been, with a lot of people filming them clinking glasses with some official looking people and everyone clapping.

Are they going to do that knocking-down thing to all the places and things they mark in red? I said.

I shouldn't think so, she said. This one's a special case. Big publicity noise.

The event across the road was over now; the

people in suits getting into the backs of a fleet of cars and being driven away, the filmers drifting off in all directions. Some people in hard hats and high-vis were rolling closed the hoarding round the empty space, others dismantling the platform.

So if they're not going to knock down all the places that they paint red round, why are they painting red round buildings at all? I said. What's the point?

I'd have said the point makes itself pretty clear. Look. Use your eyes.

The hoarding was closed now, the barriers down, pavement unblocked. People were crossing towards the station and away from it. But their communal flow altered when they got to the place where I'd upended the supera bounder the other day, where the paint had gone all over the pavement and the road. Like an electric current was magnetizing anyone who neared it away from it, the flow of people curved suddenly off and round it.

See what a simple line, a visible mark of the utmost simplicity and cheapness, can do to a populace? she said.

I watched the crowd sway like foliage in sea round submerged rockface.

She was readying herself to move on, I could feel it.

Oona, I said.

She stopped, turned towards me, head down.

She was pretending to be going through her coat pockets.

Can I trust you?

You'll have to decide that for yourself, she said.

Can you come to where I'm living? For just ten minutes?

She didn't ask why.

You go there now, I'll follow you, but in my own way. I'll knock on your door an hour after you get home, she said.

Just over an hour later I let her into the house.

She stood and looked at yesterday's piles of dung now drying on the footmat space just inside the front door.

I took her down the hall, opened the door and showed her into the back room, the one with a sink, which we were very lucky to have downstairs because of the on-tap water; horses have to drink a lot of water and I don't know what we'd have done if we'd had to get that horse up the stairs.

It was standing with its tail towards us, and its haunches, one hind leg bent, hoof pointed resting on the floorboards nonchalant, for all the world like this was its house and we were the visitors to it.

Who's this person? my sister said.

I'm a friend of Briar's, Oona said. I think I already know who you are.

How come you know anything about me? my sister said.

She was holding the horse's nose. Its nose made her hands look like a very small child's. The horse looked round at Oona and snorted. The force of the snort hit Colin's fringe. He was sitting on the floor.

That's a good sign. It likes you, Colin said to Oona.

He wiped the front of his head and looked at his hand to see what he'd wiped.

I'm Marianne Faithless, my sister said.

Not Rose, then, Oona said.

Did you tell her? my sister said to me.

Just your name, I said. Her name's Oona. She's the one and the only and her grandmother was a goddess.

Was? my sister said. Can someone stop being a goddess? Like, get out of being one?

Someone called Marianne Faithless probably could, Oona said.

She likes to name herself, sort of, after the singers from the past that our mother likes to play to us, I said.

Thank you Briar, Oona said.

Liked to play to us, my sister said. Long ago. When we all lived together in a whole other story.

Why does she keep saying your name wrong? Colin said.

Sometimes I get called one of those names, sometimes the other, I said.

Oh, he said.

He furrowed his brow and stared at me.

Right, he said.

And how about you? Oona said to him. Also the genus rosa?

The what? Colin said.

Are you family too?

I'm –, Colin said.

Then he said,

Colin.

He shot me a shy look as he said it.

Kendrick, he said.

Kendrick's Farm Goods, Oona said.

That's us, Colin said.

Colin's been helping us out by bringing food in nosebags, I said.

For Champion the wonder horse here, Oona said.

Her name's Gliff, my sister said.

It's not a mare. It's a gelding, Colin said.

Glyph? like hieroglyph? Oona said.

No, my sister said. Gliff like cliff with a G.

I heard someone had broken some horses out, Oona said. How many of them are living in this house?

Just the one we bought, my sister said.

Smells like more than one in here, Oona said.

We couldn't afford more than one, my sister said.

You've only put a deposit on it, Colin said. You've paid only roughly one fifth leaving roughly four fifths left to pay. Plus oats.

He turned to Oona.

My father's on the rampage. He'll kill whoever did it. They're loose in the woods, they'll eat poisonous things they're not supposed to eat and they'll die.

They were going to die anyway, my sister said. Now at least if they die they'll have had a chance.

They won't get enough water, Colin said to

Oona. The weather's supposed to turn crazy hot again soon.

Then it's good they're in a shady wood, my sister said.

They can't keep it here, Colin said. And they know nothing about horses. A horse is half a ton of panic on a rope.

So don't put a horse on a rope, my sister said. Then there'll be no panic, just the half a ton, and he didn't need a rope on him to get him here, did he, and there was no panic. He just came with us, walked in through the front door, like we did.

Colin looked bewildered again.

I agree. You really can't keep a horse in here, Oona said.

Plus I can't keep stealing food from home, Colin said to Oona. Someone'll notice. They'll UV me.

You keep saying that, my sister said.

He looked at us all then he looked away, looked at the wall, at nothing. He looked terrified.

Right, then, Oona said. I've seen enough of the back of a horse for now.

Surefooted like a dancer moving she sidestepped the pile of dung next to her swinging the hem of her coat up so it wouldn't brush over the top of it. She came and stood next to me, put her hand on my shoulder and asked me to show her round the rest of the house.

There aren't any more horses here, I said.

I believe you, she said. Thousands wouldn't.

She looked into the empty front room. She followed me upstairs. She saw the tins of food, the full ones and the empty ones. She picked up one of the empty meatball tins, turned it over in her hand, put it down again. She saw our rucksacks. She saw the kettle. She saw the bolt cutters leaning up against the wall. She saw the other rooms with nothing in them.

She came back into our sleeping room. She looked me up and down.

How long have you been living here? she said.

That long, I said.

I pointed to the line of opened emptied tins.

A tin a day for me, half a tin for my sister, I said.

And the boy from the farm?

Doesn't live here, I said.

She made a wise laughing sound, part comic, part warning.

No, it'll be okay, I said. He really likes Rose. We didn't even need the bolt cutters in the end. She got him to give her the padlock key. And he's stopped wearing his educator around us.

You sure? she said.

No, I said.

Ah, she said.

She sat down on the floor of our sleeping room like a young person would, crosslegged. She did a thing with her arm that meant I had to sit down too. I did.

Okay. Now. You tell me it all, the story of you so far.

Where do you want me to start? I said.

Wherever you think the start is, she said.

I started with our mother coming down to the docking gate to say cheerio to us.

power

There was once a mother who was about to give birth.

The usual people who help people give birth came round to help. But as soon as the baby's head started to come out of the mother they all ran away squealing because this baby's head wasn't the head of a baby human. It was the head of a little horse.

Other than having this head of a very small horse the baby looked completely like a baby does. At first the mother was upset. But then the baby was lying there in its crib, and looking right at her with such calm and honesty, such an open look and such lovely forward ears and whiskers, that she knew that her baby was really, really beautiful, perfect actually. She fell in love. She reached out and stroked the length of her baby's long nose. She fed her and she noticed how carefully the baby fed from her with its horse teeth.

She held her on her knee and played a game of horsey, bounced her up and down.

She called her horse headed daughter Saccobanda, after the story of a local family who'd stood up first to the bullies living next door to them, then to the town bullies who painted the red outline round their house, then to the powerful people who organized all the red paint lines in the town.

And the baby Saccobanda grew up into a lovely little girl with the head of a beautiful horse and was a joy to live with and very cheap to keep because she ate nothing but grass and oats and she never complained.

This might've been because she didn't speak at all, not a single word, just the occasional snort and nicker and neigh.

But she was calm, and gentle, and it seemed so uncannily generous when she sent a glance your way that even if she'd been a speaker of words she'd probably not have used them to complain anyway.

As Saccobanda grew older her mother also realized she had a real rare talent. Her talent was that she seemed able to hear all the things that people weren't saying or didn't say, both when they were speaking and when they were completely silent.

She could also hear what all the things round us that don't use words were saying. Like what a dog was saying, or a cat, or a bird or a firefly or a spider or aphid, and even the things which don't seem to have the same kind of life, a rockface, a pebble or a blade of grass, a tin can full of meatballs, even pieces of rubbish like an empty tin after someone's eaten the meatballs, a piece of thrown away plastic that used to be a bit of a doll,

and soon people were coming from far and wide to meet the horse with the body of a girl, the girl with the head of a horse, and some of them would even come wearing masks shaped like horse heads, from their own countries' traditions, so that sometimes Saccobanda's mother would look out of her window and see on the bench in the garden what looked like two horses in silent conversation or contemplation.

Whoever came to see Saccobanda always left happier, as if something difficult had finally been understood.

The very poor came first, the people without anything to their names. Even so they always brought gifts and although Saccobanda's mother would insist that no gifts were necessary they would still leave whatever they'd brought as offerings at the front gate, fruit or wheat, eggs or wild bee honey, fresh vegetables, hard-won olive oil.

Then some of the very rich even started coming

too. Most explained they came because they were sad and had no idea why they were sad, or what to buy to stop themselves feeling sad. Saccobanda's mother refused their offers of money and Saccobanda sat with them, glanced her glance at whoever came, all were welcome and nothing was about money or payment, it was all about what it meant just to be there, to know they were there and to glance for a moment back.

Whoever came, it didn't matter, her treatment of everybody was the same.

They would sit in silence with Saccobanda looking at them with one or the other of her gentle eyes, shaking her long head if flies landed near her eyes and waving them gently away with her little hands, and then they'd leave renewed each time, not just the people, the flies too, they'd be full of new presence like flies who'd also been seen and heard and understood.

Any and every creature round her seemed to have been recognized and to grow in stature because of it.

Rocks and stones and blades of grass, the floating fluff off dandelions, even air itself, and rivers, everything in rivers from the fish to the floating or long sunk rubbish – everything graced by her presence wherever it came into her presence, whether an empty tin can or the thrown away wrapping off a sandwich, a flake of rusty metal off a passing car, every deep layered mineral, all the leavings of every rotted and disappeared leaf.

All of it gained a meaning true to itself, near Saccobanda.

It wasn't till the people who'd declared themselves in charge decided to declare Saccobanda unverifiable and sent officials to take her away for being neither what they thought a person should be nor what they thought a horse should be, officials who looked appalled at what they'd been tasked to do, but still did it, determined, implacable, and Saccobanda with the rough rope draped round her neck went meekly and willingly with them, and never came back again, that the people who'd known her or heard about her powers and her talent realized what they'd lost.

So, led by the example of Saccobanda's mother – who never forgot her beautiful daughter, never will, is still fighting for her and always will be fighting for her – the people rose up in revolt.

Not just the people.

All the creatures did too and the rocks, the stones, the grass, the seas, the rivers, the weeds, the weeds were angry at the way they'd been treated, and the weather was furious, and the thrown away plastic yoghurt pots and water bottles, the obsolete dumped dead games and phones and fridges and wordprocessors, all the things with poisonous batteries in them, old metal, and all the old bones and the new, all the mistreated and hurt and broken people and things, the left-for-rubbish of centuries, together it all rose in fury into a mountainous clamouring and the clamouring grew and grew until it formed a great grey moving mountain that upped itself out of the ground, crossed the country and the countries as fast and as unstoppably and as naturally as a landslide, and slid to a stop only to stop up every door of every place where anyone thought they were in charge of the world.

The mountainous movement across the earth made a clamour so huge and so righteous that it gathered everything true to it, and it always will, the great grey mountain of mistreatment and misuse, and it's still doing that work for the people and the things of the world robbed of what and who they are, it's still furious at that robbery, it's still moving, still growing, still gathering even more strength and still rolling forward like an avalanche, listen, hear that rumbling noise underneath and over everything? gathering and rolling forward to wherever it's most needed?

Or:

How do you say hello to a horse? I said.

I'll show you, my sister said.

We were standing in the early morning, the air already thickening with mist, some of which seemed to be rising off the back of the horse. Someone called Arkan had cleared a patch of the playing field yesterday with a lawnmower and together the small group of people who lived here had helped us clear everything from it that might harm a horse, at least according to Colin. The makeshift fence round the cleared space was made of a lot of old classroom chairs and tables shoved up against each other in a big oblong. Two small feral looking kids, ragged, both looked about seven years old, had been told off several times for knocking some of these flimsy chairs to one side as if to let the horse out.

The strange thing about these children was that they were completely silent. They moved like lightning, racing round the school and the grounds so lightly that the sudden presence of one or other of them at my side from nowhere had made me jump already more than once. They disappeared, reappeared, disappeared again, were almost immediately two hundred yards away across the field and the next second several chairs were upside down, a desk or two knocked awry. The one of them whose name I never knew had a pair of scuffed earbuds in their ears. When I asked someone else who lived here what they were listening to all the time, she said,

they don't work, those buds, so I guess they're listening to the inside of their ears.

This morning some of the chairs were lying on their sides on the grass and the fence was full of openings. But the horse was still there in the enclosure as if perfectly happy to be there and was now coming slowly across the shorter grass towards us in the mist.

I leaned on the back of one of the still-standing chairs.

It could easy just walk out of there, I said. And it hasn't.

My sister shrugged.

I told him last thing last night I'd come and get him this morning and that we'd take him in before it got too hot today, she said.

Yeah but how much does a horse understand of what you're saying? I said. I mean what did it, what did he, *really* know when you were telling him that?

You say hello like this, she said.

She stretched her arm out as the horse came near, her hand held towards the tip of its nose.

Not that he doesn't also hear when you use words, she said. Hello Gliff.

The horse put its – his – nose into her hand. Even though there were already several possible ways through the furniture fence my sister shifted the two chairs directly in front of us so the horse could come out through the opening she made, and he did, came walking beside us all the way across the high dry grass to the building then over the old car park space, the tarmac already softening underfoot this early under the sun, then easily up the broad school steps and in.

The noise of him even just slow-walking inside the building rang above us like weird magic all through the corridor and into the big hall.

You stay here with him while I sort this, my sister said.

Real grey horse, swaying his shoulders, tail flicking beneath the massive picture hung above the stage. Bright horse, shadowy lion. I wished I'd been cleverer when Ulyana was talking about this picture to us, as clever as my sister. I wished I'd said, I imagined myself now saying,

but Ulyana, the lion's looking at the artist as if the artist's stupid, like the lion's saying, why are you giving my friend the horse here such a hard time? Back off. Right now.

I pulled myself up to sit on the edge of the stage under the picture, swung my legs, watched the real horse just standing in all the empty space shifting his weight from hoof to hoof, head low to the parquet. My sister went back and fore between here and the toilets bringing half-pailfuls of water one on each arm and pouring them into the things the people here had given us: a plastic bucket found in a cleaning cupboard, the plastic hood of the lawnmower, two large plastic storage tubs that looked like recycling bins. My sister was dutiful. The hall was cool and still. The horse stood, closed his eyes in what morning light came through the glass of the rusty skylights in the roof. One skylight was broken. Below it, all down the wall, all the way to the floor, was the stain of past rain.

This was a room from when children, in the old days, all learned things at once together in one building. I closed my eyes, tried to imagine people here learning things in these rooms all at the same time.

The people who lived here now were:

Oona.

Valentina Mini and her friend Arkan; they were in charge of the fence and the upkeep of things.

Ulyana, who knew about the sublime.

A thin clever man called Bertin; he was missing a finger on one hand. He said he'd caught it in a fence underwater and had had to choose whether to leave it behind or drown.

The girl who'd called me a cat and told me the big dogs would get me. Her name was Daisy.

A fifteen year old boy called Wolf whose job description, my sister and I decided, was to be as sullen as possible.

The two wild silent children with the ragged clothes and hair, one was called Little, and I never found out the other's name.

Oona. Valentina. Arkan. Ulyana.

Dobbin. Pegasus. Gliff.

Why was it different calling a person something from calling a horse a name? It *was* different, subtly different, but subtly the same too. I'd never thought about it before, and why did I myself really like having more than one name, as if I had more than one self? Why were my sister and I so careful and keen to evade when we told people our names? Evade what? Why did we so often naturally know to tell them names that weren't our names at all, and why did doing this leave us reeling with happiness, and was any of this related to saying hello to a horse? Or giving a horse as a name just some word, a meaningless word like gliff, from then on supposed to mean that individual horse whether the horse knew it or not?

Last night Oona'd ushered us in to what said on the door it was a Headmaster's Office, we were carrying our rucksacks and kitchen stuff and what was left of our cans. It had been a badge of honour, us arriving complete with a horse. It had made us unusually interesting.

This is Briar, also known as Brice, and this is Rose of Allendale.

That's not my name, my sister'd said to the room.

Then my sister and I had been made to sit on the most comfortable seats in the place and were given so much food to eat we couldn't finish all of it.

Afterwards Oona had sung an old song about clear fair mornings, a calm sea, somebody at your side when you go wandering. There were a lot of flowers in the song, it was a song about flowers really, and about somebody whose name wasn't Rose but who becomes a kind of symbolic rose to the singer. The singer is a person who's been east and west and never been alone because of this rose coming with them wherever they are. When the singer's boat is wrecked by sea storms, the rose alone withstands the storms. When the singer is fevered and thirsty in desert sand, the rose keeps the singer alive by telling them stories of all the other possible places, all the happinesses. At the end the singer says their life would have been nothing if they hadn't had the Rose of Allendale in their life.

I take it back, my sister'd said when she heard it. I *am* Rose of Allendale.

Everybody except the small children raised their cups and glasses to Brice/Briar and Rose of Allendale. It was embarrassing, but also lovely, like we had a brightness round us, like we might really matter to a room full of people we didn't know, and Oona'd sung that song with an unfussy voice that sounded as sturdy as a well-made wooden table and it was the first time I'd understood that the thought of an ordinary wooden table could itself be a kind of comfort. Her voice was a shock, the sound so young coming out of the elderly figure she seemed to be. It was like everything you thought you knew could be rewritten.

Like learning that time can sing and that it's old *and* young, I'd whispered.

Stop saying words, my sister'd whispered back. I want to hear the story.

At the end the girl I'd made laugh about the catflap came over to speak to me.

You got in, then, she'd said. I'm Daisy, and which of those many names she told us are you?

Which would you like me to be? I said.

Nice of you to offer me a choice, she said, and are you a boy or a girl?

Yes I am, I said.

Okay, she said, well, that's either very brave of you or very stupid, given recent developments in history, so which is it?

You're missing the point, I said.

She gave me a measuring look then she laughed and shook her head.

You're more trouble than it's worth, she said.

They took us to another room on the ground floor, it said Nurse's Office on the door. They gave us clean bedding and made us up beds that were quite like real beds, one up on high legs, one on the floor, with pillows and such. I'd slept properly last night for the first time since Leif had gone. The water in this building could be hot too, and was plentiful. There were showers that still worked. We were clean again. We'd eaten rice, cheese, actual vegetables; lucky for my sister who'd eaten nothing but sweetcorn for the last couple of days the people here made real food in what had once been rooms where young people were taught how to make meals, where some ovens and hobs still worked, at least when the electricity was working. Valentina always knew how to get it working again and her friend Arkan who had a beard so long he tied it up in a knot at the top of his head to keep it out of the way when he was working or eating was always sorting the rubble where bits of the building had fallen in on themselves and trying to make it watertight before the big storms came, they were coming soon, they always did after the heat.

We could stay until we were ready to move on, Ulyana had told us last night. Could we shelter the horse from the sun somewhere? Yes, in what was called the assembly hall. But when we'd seen it with its good wooden floor we'd exchanged glances with each other. My sister had said two words.

Horsepiss. Horseshit.

Valentina had laughed and said,

we don't care! We never use this room.

She'd pointed at the picture above the stage of the horse and the lion.

We'll christen it Horse Hall at the first piss, she said.

She'd sent Arkan and Bertin to try to track down straw for the floor. There was none here yet. I was hoping they'd bring it soon because horsepiss would spread everywhere in here. It was amazing how much horses could piss, and how they did it, stretching themselves to keep their own hooves well out of the way of what came out of them.

All the people living here, including the feral children, were right now unverifiables. They were largely unverifiable because of words. One person here had been unverified for saying out loud that a war was a war when it wasn't permitted to call it a war. Another had found herself declared unverifiable for writing online that the killing of many people by another people was a genocide. Another had been unverified for defaming the oil conglomerates by saying they were directly responsible for climate catastrophe. Another had been unverified for speaking at a protest about people's right to protest.

The ferals had been marked unverifiable simply because nobody knew what had happened to their adults and it couldn't be proved who they were.

Unverifiable unverifiable unverifiable.

I thought of us in the worded world.

I looked at the horse.

By standing in this wide room meant for something else altogether the horse brought something of another possible world into the place.

Was a horse more lost to the world, because of no words, or was the horse more found – or even founded – in the world because of no words?

Were we in our worded world the ones who were truly deluded about where and what we believed about all the things we had words for?

My sister came back, water slopping. The buckets she was carrying made her look even smaller.

I jumped down to help.

I've got it, she said. I'm doing it.

What's the point? I said.

Colon told us. Water, then more water. After that, more water. And when you think you've probably fetched as much water as he needs, get even more water. Horses need a lot of water. And Colon said that we might have to sponge him down with cool water too if he starts sweating and deep breathing or gets unsteady on his feet in the heat.

No. I mean what's the point in calling a horse a name? I said.

She looked at me like I was speaking a language she didn't understand.

He's mine, she said. Ours. We've bought him. We're buying him. We can call him what we like.

Yeah, but is that what a name is? Another word for ownership? When really you giving our money to a boy who says he or his father or whoever owns this horse, well, it doesn't really make this horse, if we look at it from the horse's world view, any more *their* horse, *your* horse or *our* horse, I said.

What's another word for mad? she said.

Deranged? I said.

You're deranged, she said.

But isn't you thinking you can own it, or him, and call him a name, sort of deranged too? and isn't it in fact exactly the same in some ways as the other people who'll have called him other names before in his lifetime and thought they could decide what to do with his life, ride him, treat him well or badly, send him to a slaughterhouse?

My sister rolled her eyes.

Uh huh. Whatever, she said.

She left the room with the empty pails on her arm.

Soon everybody else in the place would wake up and this hall would be full of the people who lived here coming to hang out with what they all called our horse.

I went and stood closer to the, our, horse.

I'm Bri. I'm deranged. More trouble than it's worth, I said. What are you?

He opened one eye at me then shut it again, lowered his head, breathed out wetly right on to me.

I wiped my arm on the leg of my jeans. I remembered that Colin, when the horse had made a noise like this in our kitchen, had said horses do that when they like someone, that this noise had meant something approving.

But just because Colin had said this it didn't mean the noise meant what he'd said it did.

You don't need a name, do you? I said.

He didn't, any more than the dog we called Rogie that'd lived with us for a time then vanished, presumably gone on with his life elsewhere while we went on with ours without him, was ever really anything to do with the name we'd called him.

So there was the word that made the name, and there was the dog that it conjured in the mind, and there, way beyond it, totally free of it himself, was the real dog, wagging or not wagging his tail.

It was me who was tethered to the word.

I looked at the veins running under the skin above and below the horse's eye all the way down his cheekbone.

What's horse world like? I said.

His mouth was decisive without force, a soft lipped line. It made him look resigned, noncommittal, but also poised, as if waiting.

What for?

I heard it in my head in my sister's voice. *Deranged*. *Whatever*. The horse swung his head away, swung it back towards me without looking at me, shook his mane lightly, lowered his head, settled again.

What do you make of your new field? Better than being in the house. Or in here. At least here there's room to move. We have to keep you out of the sun but you'll be able to go back out late today when it cools, and be out at night, and we're sorting horse food for in here, I mean feed, as well as the grass you can eat out there, and we're working out how to pay for it. We don't know what we're going to do, or how. But we're going to do it.

The horse stood, indifferent. It was like I'd said nothing.

What's a horse day like? I said. What's it like being a horse at night, can you see in the dark, like cats, and owls? What was it like last night in that moonlight? What's it like if you're out in a field and it starts to rain? Do you mind? Does it feel good? Unpleasant? Does horsehair keep the rain off? Do you prefer it when it's cold out? Or hot? Can you feel heat, like, did you feel the heat on the tarmac when we came in, can you feel it up through your hooves? Do hooves feel? What was your life like before us? Where were you born? Do you remember being born? What are horse memories like? Where did you live? Who was your mother? What was she like? Who was your father? Do horses care about fathers, or mothers? Do horses have family, I mean like me and my sister, and my mother and her sister? How come you ended up in that abattoir field on Colin's farm? Who owned you and did that to you? I mean, who thought they owned you?

Nothing.

Gliff, I said.

I said it to see how it felt.

I patted his neck like my sister had shown me how to.

Good Gliff, I said.

Someone in the art hotel answered speaking in their other language.

Something something something?

I said in my own language,

hello, I wonder if you can help me.

The person spoke back to me in my language and it struck me how near miraculous it seemed – and how ordinary it must be for whoever can do it – for someone to be able to shift from one language to another in a split second.

I was in a big darkened room up on the first floor. It had a sign saying Language Lab on the door. It had several neat but scuffed rows of booths with what looked like volume controls and old fashioned headphones whose rubber had perished, and at the front of the room a couple of computers from prehistory.

The girl called Daisy was monitoring me.

What's it for? she said next morning when I asked about the phone.

I told her about Leif, and about our mother. She nodded, grave but disengaged, like it was a story she was used to hearing, and said,

you can have ninety seconds.

She got a phone out of a drawer, switched it on, pressed some buttons, handed me it. It was one of the old kind of phones that only drug dealers used to have, the kind that didn't take photos or access the net.

Does this even still work? I said.

When we're lucky, she said.

My sister was standing at the open door.

Can she come in and speak to them too? I said.

Nope.

Why?

Daisy went over and shut the door. She explained the rules. Only one person at a time allowed into the Language Lab. She was in charge of who got to use the phone and she always stayed in the room to make sure whoever used it wasn't calling anyone they shouldn't. This was for the good of the community.

I'm not going to hurt the community! I said.

That's what the last person who hurt the community said. Ninety seconds is all you've got in any one call. Otherwise they can trace us. Okay. Ready? Go.

Leif's number.

It was now more than a week since he'd left us in the house so I thought it wasn't too impolite to ask if he'd be back soon. I pressed the buttons and put the phone to my ear.

You have reached a number that has been disconnected or is no longer in service. If you feel you have reached this recording in error please check the number and call again.

I called it again. Then again.

Can I text on this? I said.

Daisy got the text page up for me.

Message failed.

Hmm, she said.

Can my ninety seconds start again please? I said.

Hurry up, she said.

I tried Alana's number. It rang at the other end like a phone should. I pictured it ringing somewhere on the bed in her shaded flat, I thought of her face small and pale, placed at the top of the bedcovers like a head that had no body beneath it at all.

But the phone rang and rang. No answer. No answerphone.

The hotel, then.

I am sorry. There is nobody of that name here.

Not like staying, or a guest or anything, I mean working for you, I said. In the restaurant. And cleaning the rooms.

The staff cannot be reached by phoning this number.

Can you tell me the number to use to speak to the staff please?

The staff cannot be reached.

It's an emergency, I said.

I am sorry.

Well, can I leave a message for her please?

One moment. I will check the staff list for the name. Please hold.

[Pause.]

Through the little glass window high in this room's door I watched the top of my sister's head.

Hello? No, I am sorry. There is nobody of that name working here.

I gave the person on the phone Alana's name instead.

[Pause.]

My sister was too small to see through the glass in the door but she was listening, pressed hard against it, I could hear her shifting against the wood.

Hello? Again I am sorry. There is nobody of that name working here.

Can you just check the list one more time for me? I said. Because she was definitely there a week ago. Alana works there like all the time usually but she's been ill so she was covering Alana's shifts for her. She looks a bit like Alana. You all maybe just thought she was Alana.

[Pause.]

Hello? I am sorry but there is no people with these names on the list of who is working or worked here.

There must be, I said. We saw her. Last week. We were there. She was there. She was wearing Alana's clothes.

I am sorry. I cannot help you further.

I held the dead phone in my hand.

Daisy regarded me with something not unlike sympathy.

Can I just check some things on that computer? I said. To see if there's any other way?

I don't know how to work it, Daisy said. It's older than me.

I'm good at tech, I said.

Yeah but check how many things? Daisy said.

Two minutes, I said.

She bunched her mouth up into a frown. But she came over and watched as I opened one of them and worked out what to press to get the web up.

Daisy went over to stand at the boarded-up window with her back to me.

Ninety seconds, she said. No more.

I keyed in the name of the hotel. The hotel's page came up, an image of the outside of it and an image of the restaurant. There, that was the docking gate, with the pointless candles and the rigor mortis art.

The images were full of strangers. They looked photoshopped on. Certainly there was nothing of my mother, or Alana, or any staff, anyone wearing the clothes we knew the staff had to wear there.

I closed the link.

I keyed in Leif's name.

But I didn't know his surname.

I erased him. I keyed in the first three letters of our mother's name.

I heard her voice in my head as I did it. *Bri. Don't be stupid. Why do you think they call it a net? Why do you think they call it a web?*

I erased the three letters one after the other. Daisy cast me a hurry up look. I didn't want it to seem like I was a loser or that I'd wasted precious resource or time so I frowned down at the screen as if I were reading something very important.

My sister, waiting on the other side of the door.

I keyed in the word *gelding*.

A male horse is often gelded to make him better-behaved and easier to control. Gelding can also remove lower-quality animals from the gene pool. To allow only the finest animals to breed on, while preserving adequate genetic diversity, only a small percentage of all male horses should remain stallions.

I keyed in the word *dictionaries*, then into a dictionary search bar the word *gliff*.

I expected pretty much nothing.

I expected it to say *no listing for this word* or *meaningless nonsense word*.

Uh, Daisy? I said.

Finish now, she said. Or else.

Can I borrow something to write on? I said. And something to write with? And does anyone in this building have access to a dictionary I can look at for longer than ninety seconds?

You want the world on a string while you're at it? Daisy said.

She switched the computer off.

Come with me. I'll pass you over to someone who can actually meet your needs.

It said Library on one of the swing doors. Oona gently pushed the door a little open. The boards on the outsides of this room's windows let in light round their edges. All over the front of the building they'd been trimmed back slightly to do this and still leave the windows looking boarded up.

What I could see was a broad room. Then my eyes made out the books.

Books everywhere.

So many books, more books than I'd ever seen all in one place. The backs of books, in rows that reached up to the ceiling, books and books and books, at every level, high and low, piles of them, shelf after shelf of them.

Wherever my eye went, books.

Oh! I said.

Oona spoke very quietly next to me.

Back when this was still a school, she said, this was my first employment.

In here? I said. Looking after books? Is that a job? That people can do?

It was, she said. Who taught you and Rose to read?

Our mother, I said.

You've been lucky, she said.

She took me by the shoulders and guided me in and we stood at the front of the room. She spoke to the room, hushed but clear, in case anyone else happened to be reading in here – or maybe she was addressing the books themselves – saying,

this one wants to look at the dictionaries and promises to be quiet while doing it. Don't you?

Yes! I said,

and the word came out of me like an excited squeak.

There wasn't just a dictionary or a couple of dictionaries in this room. There was a whole wall of dictionaries. They were huge. I had thought that a dictionary was something roughly the size of an average mother's hand. I had never thought to imagine so many different makes and sizes of dictionary, or that one single dictionary split into several volumes could take up several long shelves on a wall.

Oona tore a wedge of pages out of her notebook and gave them to me. She took my hand, took me to the table at the back of the room, took a pencil out of her pocket, broke it in half, put the broken end into a box attached by a clamp to the table, turned its handle and took the piece of pencil out sharp pointed.

She showed me how to empty the little tray of sharpened-off bits of wood into a waste bin.

I picked a stray piece of it off the old carpet, put its zigzag to my nose. This was definitely one of my best moments. I thought of my sister and the day she'd fed the horse the grass. Later, I decided, I'd go to the part of the building with the cookery rooms in it and see if Bertin, who cooked the food for us, still had our last tin of creamed rice among the tins we'd not opened. I'd get him to open it for me and I'd bring it back to the room they'd given us so my sister and I could share it tonight.

Here, Oona said.

She took me over to the seat with the most light hitting it, at the corner of the table next to the dictionary wall.

This is your designated place in here whenever you want while you're at St Saccobanda's, she said. And over here, at your back, this is our pitifully small I'm afraid collection of dictionaries in different languages.

There are dictionaries for other languages here too? I said.

You can learn some of those languages, if you want, she said, while you're here. I'll teach you.

What, for speaking? I said. To people?

You've no idea the doors that open when a word in one language crosses into another language, she said.

Is there a dictionary that will help us speak to a horse? I said.

Most humans haven't got clever enough to speak the languages of other creatures yet for some reason, she said. I often wonder why. Does it make it easier to control other creatures, or even peoples, us deciding that because we don't know what they're saying, what they're saying doesn't get to mean anything, or that they don't get to have a say?

There's a language on the front of the school, I said. Facta sunt ipse verba.

Ah. Now there I *can* help you, she said.

She went to the dictionary shelves, pulled one out.

Have a good time, she said. I sense you will.

She swung out through the swing doors. I sat down in the smell of hot wood and leather and paper.

Facta.

Noun, 2nd declension neuter, plural: facts, deeds, acts, achievements.

Sunt.

Verb, present tense, third person plural: from the verb to be, or to exist.

Ipse.

Pronoun: himself, herself, itself. The very real/actual one. In person. Themselves.

Verba.

Noun, 2nd declension neuter, plural: word, proverb, idiomatic construction [verba dare alicui => to cheat/deceive someone].

Okay. So. Words themselves are facts, deeds, acts, achievements? or facts, deeds, acts and achievements themselves are words?

Pacta.

Noun, 2nd declension neuter, plural: bargain, agreement, manner. Words themselves are bargains, agreements, manners. Bargains, agreements, manners themselves are words?

Iacta.

From the verb 'iacere', 3rd conjugation: to throw away, throw out, jerk about, disturb, boast, discuss. I had no idea what that would mean. Words themselves are being thrown away? Words themselves are boasts? Boasts themselves are words? The thrown away things are words?

Tacta.

From the verb 'tangere', 3rd conjugation: to touch, strike, influence, touch on. Words themselves are a kind of touching? Words themselves are influence? Words themselves are a form of hitting? Or the other way round? Striking or touching is all about words?

It was thrilling to me to sit and try to piece it together, even if I was wrong. I knew what proverbs were. But what was idiomatic? and how was it anything to do with construction?

I looked up the word *idiomatic* in a different dictionary. Thrilling to me, the variety. Thrilling both to know and to not know, to be gifted possibilities, thrilling above all to see for myself the ways the words on the front of the school building might be related to words we used but at the same time weren't them.

Like there was such a thing as a family of words, one that stretched across different languages all touching on each other, hitting or striking each other, acting on each other, influencing each other, agreeing with each other or throwing each other out, disturbing each other, doing all of these things at once.

What gliff means:

a short moment. A momentary resemblance. A sudden or chance view. A transient glance. A sudden fright. A faint trace or suggestion. An inkling. A wink of sleep. A slight attack or touch of illness. A whiff. A puff. A sudden perceptible smell. A sudden passing sensation either of pain or of pleasure. A scare. A shock. A thrill. A sudden violent blow. A wallop. A nonsense word. A misspelling for glyph. A substitute word for any word. A synonym for spliff. A post-ejaculatory sex act. A mood someone's partner gets in when they miss their partner too much and get upset about it. An organization that works for drug abuse prevention in Vienna. A brand name for an early AI tech tool used in the development of healthcare. A character in something called

Ninjago. A rumour. An impulse. An instant. An unexpected view of something that startles you. A state of nervous disposition. A sudden surprising fall of sunlight.

The twinkling of an eye.

To glimpse. To frighten. To be abruptly seized with fear. To look at someone or something in an unheeding or hurried or careless manner. To glint. To gleam. To glare. To flare.

To strike a glancing blow at someone or something.

To evade or escape something quickly.

To glimmer like sudden unanticipated light.

To dispel snow.

You got through to nobody, then? my sister said.
Nobody who could help, I said.
Even at the hotel?
You heard me through the door, I said.
And you tried Alana's?
I nodded, shook my head.
Oh, she said.
We looked at each other.
We have to go home, I said. She'll come back and not know where to find us. Maybe she's already there. Maybe she's sitting in the front room wondering where we are right now. Oh. And also. I found out what a gelding is for you.
I don't care what kind of horse he is, she said.
It's a lot to do with behaviour, and control, and what's called good breeding as opposed to poor breeding, apparently. And. Also. I got you this.

I handed her the folded piece of paper with all the meanings written out on it.

She unfolded it and read it.

Some of them I'm not so sure about, they were online definitions, urban definitions, I said. I think a lot of rubbish happens online. But still, a meaning's a meaning. And see, listen, you've actually called him something unpindownable. Something really excitingly polysemous. At least, exciting to me.

Something what the what? she said.

Polysemous. I looked that word up too. I wanted to find a word that meant what you've done.

What is it I've done? she said frowning and looking at the unfolded page.

You've named him a word that doesn't just mean so many things, it can also mean all of them *and* none of them at once.

I pointed to the list.

And even more – one of its meanings is, here, see? –

a substitute word for any word

– you've given him a name that can stand in for, or represent, any other word, any word that exists. Or ever existed. Or will. Because of what you called him, he can be everything and anything. And at the same time his name can mean nothing at all. It's like you've both named him *and* let him be completely meaning-free!

Oh, she said. Right.

She nodded, but upwards instead of downwards, chin up, head back, like a movement a horse that didn't want to be haltered would make.

Thanks, she said.

She folded the piece of paper up and put it in her back pocket.

Was it laughter? It was coming from the two small children who never made much noise of any kind, so it was doubly surprising. They were standing together on one of the chairs that made up the fence round the horse and they were watching Wolf, who'd taken a chair himself, had dragged it over to where the horse was and was using it to climb up on to the horse's back. We watched him do it and we watched the horse rear gently up so he slid straight off backwards and down on to the grass again. The two small children made the same noise.

Yes. It was their version of laughter.

Little held seven fingers up to me in a triumphant way.

Seventh time? I said.

Little made the strange gurgle again and turned back to watch Wolf try one more time, put the chair down, get up on the chair, sling himself over the horse's back and the horse lowered his head as far as it'd go and shook his head and whole body and Wolf slid down his neck and fell off over his head.

Then the two small children re-erected the fence so that they could jump from chair to desk to chair to chair all the way round, which again they did without making any sound other than the noise they made when they landed on one or other piece of furniture, and Wolf gave up trying.

Daisy and Wolf and my sister and I all sat on the stone at the front of the building still sunwarm under us even though it was getting dark now. They'd been out stealing anything growing that'd be edible from the greenhouse of one of the big houses across on the hilly side of town and had walked back along the river. On their way they'd seen crouched on the grass very near the riverbank what looked like a man with wings. No, not wings, just one big spread wing off to the side of him. As they got closer they saw that it was a man down on his haunches with his arms round a swan. It was cradled in his arms and between his legs. Its head rested on his shoulder and its beak was bright yellow on his sleeve.

If one of you kids just very gently, being careful not to come too close and spook my friend here, could move that thing there a little closer to my hand? he'd said.

There was a medical looking box near his foot, just too far. So Daisy picked up the box and put it where the man could reach it. The man didn't move his free hand yet. He asked them to open it for him. Wolf unclasped the tiny plastic catch from its hook and the box sprang open, bandages, syringes in plastic, sachets, things in little vials. The man said thank you.

They asked what had happened to the swan. The man said it'd broken its leg.

They asked how.

Mystery, the man said.

The swan leg, they told us, was resting motionless on the man's leg. It was like the furthest opposite thing possible to feathers and to swan whiteness, Daisy told us, the foot a huge grey-blue dark thing with webfolds hanging off it and claws at the end of them like a massive bat, and the leg itself looked scaly, like chicken-skin, and had veins like something really ancient at the same time as looking like it came from a futuristic fantasy.

They asked what would happen to it now.

The man said he'd take it to his place to make it better.

Then all the way back, Daisy complained now to us, Wolf had hounded her with information about people attacking swans. For some reason he knew an astounding amount about swan hatred. Under tonight's clear sky stars Daisy called him a swan pervert and said never in her life till then had she connected swans with the thought of people hurting swans.

That's because you're a naive, Wolf told her.

Why would anyone anywhere ever want to hurt a swan? my sister said.

You're a naive too. You can see just by looking at them, Wolf said. They look like they own it. They look like they can't be had. They look like a challenge. And they're edible. And they're protected by law. Royal decree. That stuff makes people go crazy.

Yeah but that man didn't hurt that swan. He wasn't hurting it. That man was helping that swan, Daisy said.

Maybe, Wolf said. Maybe he was going to eat it when he got home.

Then they both told us about some of the unverifiables who'd come and gone from here since they'd arrived here themselves.

My sister turned to Wolf.

What were you made unverifiable for?

He ignored the question. Instead he started singing in a pretend Oona voice a song where the singer is going crazy for love and wants Daisy to give him the answers. Daisy told him to fuck off. He told her he knew she wanted him and said something about having a bicycle that could carry two people. Daisy told us there were times when she hated her name.

I know some things about the flower you're named after, my sister said.

You don't even know it's a weed, not a flower, I said.

Weeds are just flowers or plants that people have decided to call weeds because people decide they don't want them there, my sister said. So. It's a flower.

She turned to Daisy.

It's called a daisy because it means the day's eye and it's called that because daisies open when it's light and close when it's dark.

It is *not*, I said. They do not,

because it was me who knew and cared about flowers, not her.

Then I thought to myself,

oh. They do.

And the petals are like eyelashes, she was saying. And every daisy is made up not just of one flowerhead but of really loads of little flowerheads, so there's a bunch of tiny flowers in every single small flower.

Uh huh but they named me after a song, not the flower, Daisy said. Because it was a song important in human history for being the first song ever sung by a computer programmed to sing a song by itself. IBM.

What's IBM? my sister said.

An inflammatory disease of the gut instinct, Daisy said. For which there's no cure.

Why were we unverifiable? my sister said to me now. What was it that we did?

I shrugged.

We should just go home and paint out the red round our house and go back in, she said.

Yeah. But what would happen to people if they were caught doing something like that?

Daisy bared her teeth.

What do you think happened to the people who lived here for a while and then didn't? she said.

What? I said.

Nobody answered.

The only sound came from Little and the other small child jumping and landing from wooden thing to wooden thing.

One day, my sister said, Bri, who is really good with machines and tech, is going to invent a technology that eats all the data that exists about people online so people can be free of being made to be what data says they are.

I am? I said.

Yeah, and then you're going to invent a technology that means you can stop surveillance following people who are travelling from one place to another, because that surveillance isn't anything to do with the real journeys people have to make in the world. And we're going to call that technology Campervan.

Yep, I said. And we'll call the tech that eats all the saved data Colon.

Colon and Campervan, my sister said. They're the future. We're the future. It is this simple.

From over in the enclosure the high breathy sound of the horse. My sister sat up. She got to her feet.

Wolf scowled. Eight times he'd got up on to the back of the horse. Eight times he'd been bucked or thrown off.

What can I say? my sister said. He's a one person horse. And the person's not you.

You be careful, Daisy said to her. Wandering around a field in the dark. Child's life's as brief as a candle.

You can talk, my sister said. You're only sixteen. And a candle can last a long time. Years. Decades. A whole life.

She started off, then stopped and turned.

Especially if you don't actually light it, she said.

The next day was the day Daisy went.

She and Wolf had gone to the supermarkets to scan bins for food. Someone working at one of the supermarkets told Wolf he'd seen people drive into the car park and pick her up. Literally up off the ground. They put her in the back of their van and closed its doors and they drove away.

To where? to what?

This was all we could get out of Wolf who was gaunt and dark and shaking.

We sat in the Headmaster's Office and Ulyana served up food that nobody ate, not even the two small children who were sitting glassy and blasted between Arkan and Bertin.

Where will she be? I said again. Can we go and get her back?

Valentina shook her head at me, not like she was

saying no to what I said, more like she was saying I should stop saying anything.

It happens, Oona said.

Her eyes were dark and she looked older.

That evening my sister and I went back one last time through the fence to the house that Leif had left us in.

How do you know all that stuff about daisies? I said as soon as we were off the school grounds.

Why are you such a walking question mark? she said to me. You even walk like a question mark would walk if it was a person. I know because our mother told me and I listened. Where were you when we were meant to be listening?

We opened the door with the keys on the happy children keyring and I wrote right next to where the snib was, a place you'd not miss seeing it, in case Leif came back and we weren't there, the number of the phone kept in the school Language Lab.

There's no point. He's never coming here again, my sister said looking round.

I ignored her. I wrote the word LEIF next to the number.

Nothing but a lot of dried horseshit if he does, she said. Children turned into dung.

We locked the door very carefully again to keep that house with no one and nothing in it safe and we went back through the catflap bit of the fence to the school.

I spent the evening in the library. I decided I'd try to find, in what books existed in there that were about words and their histories, whether there was a connection between the word read and the word ready.

When my sister came to get me from the library the next morning I was tucked in the corner with my head on a shelf, asleep on a paperback copy of a novel called Man in the Holocene, written by someone called, I can't remember now, something that sounded like a coffee, or a deodorant, something like Max Fresh.

I took that paperback book with me when we left. I put it in the pocket of my rucksack.

I can still see it now in my head in the wastepaper bin in the room they take me to, and the keys with the keyring with the picture of the children in the garden on it, I can feel them as if in my hand, and now the shock of the moment of the man who takes the paperback book out of my rucksack, looks at it with disregard and drops it in, takes the keys out of the rucksack and drops them in too. Then he changes his mind. He delves down, brings the book back up to his face, opens it and reads from it. *Novels are no use at all on days like these*, he reads aloud, then he laughs and says, you can say that again mate, and drops it back into the bin. He fishes out the keys, has another look at them, takes the photo of the children out of the plastic and puts it on the desk next to the screen, tells his colleague to do a facial check on it in case. Then he drops the keys back into the bin again too.

When I have access to data, later, not long after I've been verified and awarded and have worked out how to scout the system without anyone knowing what I'm doing, I pull up everyone registered called Daisy, I don't know a surname. One Daisy, about the same age as she will have been, is ARC-registered on a date roughly a week after she disappears, and is placed at a centre in the far west.

No further data.

This can be a good thing. It can be a bad thing.

In the end they bulldoze St Saccobanda's. They build a gated estate on the place where it was. According to the online catalogue and sales visuals it has fountains, colonnades, excellent security.

Over the years that I've had access I've tried to find out what happened to the other people I remember meeting there.

There's no data record of an Oona McCool at all anywhere in the system.

This can be a very good thing.

I can see from our records that our mother was refused re-entry at border control here a total of twenty seven times. I can see a birth date for her and also a death date. The re-entry attempts cease the same year of the given death date.

Death dates are not always true.

Nothing in data records is anything other than data verifiable, or ever tells you much about what really happens, or happened.

There's no data record at all for my sister.

I don't know what happens to the horse.

My sister, shaking me awake that morning to get me to look out of the window of the library with her through the space between the boards over the windows.

The sun not yet up, the horse silently nosing the grass.

There, far over at the iron fence near where the passage through to the street was, I could just see the stunted figure of a boy.

Colin? I said.

Colon, my sister said.

He had both his arms in the air and was waving them wildly, as if at us.

What is that sound? is what Leif had said in the night in the car park of the supermarket when something unthinkable woke him then woke us.

Spindly, cheap, high pitched, very offtune, the sound of one supera bounder was insidious enough to let you know that something foul was about to happen.

This time again we heard it before we saw it. Oona turned and swore, put her hands over her ears.

We were on the street side of the iron fencing, we were shifting the sheet of metal to get the horse back out; we turned and watched as row after row of supera bounders, an army of them, massed together at the turn of the road and stopped, the noise stopped, their pushers left their machines and clustered round a man holding a screen who called out numbers and street co-ordinates then sent them back to the machines and the noise started up again spooking the horse on the other side of the fence, I could hear my sister trying to calm him.

When they came through the bulge in the metal I saw she'd got her hands on his ears, she was up on the horse's back and was leaning as far forward on his neck as she could, she was speaking to him. We'd bent back the corrugate only just enough; she grazed one of her legs on the metal, she didn't care, held a hand down towards me. Get on, she said.

That horse won't let you both on, Colin said. He's way too gliffy for that.

Then Oona, so frail-seeming and stronger than any of us, came from nowhere with her arms under my arms and shunted me into the air.

Leg up, she said. There. Hold on to your sister.

No way, Colin said. They'll need a bridle.

My sister had her hands deep in the mane and I was holding on to her all right, I was trying not to slip about as the horse stepped backwards and forwards in the stupid machine noise. But it was Colin who was shouting now, oh no no no, because one machine was already closing in on us with Oona thumping its pusher in the back and on the shoulders. Then three men pulled Oona off him and sent her spinning towards the fence, which she hit and fell against, and fell down.

The horse was dancing and shying, the man with the apparatus was circling it close to the horse's feet. Now there was red paint on the outer sides of all four hooves and even up the horse's legs, there was paint dripping off the little tufts of hair behind the raised front hoof I could see, the horse had his head and his ears thrown back and now it was the pusher who looked scared of the horse, who was advancing on the supera bounder with his head thrown so far back we could see his eyes roll, he was stepping his haughtiest step, teeth bared, now he was making a noise bigger and angrier than a cough, something unbelievable from a horse, a furious roar I felt through my whole body, and Colin was shouting at the pusher now,

get away from that horse, he's not been paid for yet, you can't impound that horse, he belongs to my father,

then standing helpless and holding snapped glasses on to his face with his hand as the pusher turned and circled him instead, ran right over one of his feet with a wheel,

oh God, he was shouting, he's done me, I've been done,

as the man pushing the machine backed away from us and aimed it straight for Oona picking herself up off the ground.

The horse snorted. He stepped forward over the red paint round him like it wasn't there, one hoof in the air then down. Then the next, the next, the next.

Go on, Gliff, my sister said.

We left Colin behind as if frozen, the red circle round him, Oona up on her feet kicking at the machine and shouting at Colin to step over the line,

go on, Kendrick boy, lift your foot, *lift* it, it's nothing, it's just a line of paint, you can step out of it, right over it, there's nothing stopping you, that's it, don't be scared, go on!

It's hard to stay on a trotting horse when you don't know how to. I hung on and bounced around perilous to all three of us. We left red hoofprints for half the length of the street then fainter and fainter. Then at one point I looked round and there was no red trail behind us at all. The noise behind us faded too, the horse slowed to a walk and I began to breathe again. Soon the only noise around us was the noise of horse hoof on tarmac.

Then I realized that it smells great, being up on a horse.

I don't know how else to describe it. It smells like something *should* smell.

It's also unexpectedly rhythmic, like an extra heartbeat.

How does he know which way to go? I said.

Tell him with my legs and feet, my sister said.

The horse turned to the left. Then the horse turned to the right.

Did you do that? I said. How do you know to do that?

Easy. I'm an animal, she said.

We stayed on the horse till we got to the station where I slid off and walked around for several minutes like my legs had a barrel between them. A man was opening the doors at the front of the station building. My sister went over to ask him if he could help us with some water, and he did; he found us a bucket, filled it in their toilet block then came back out with it.

Not every day you see a horse here, he said. I used to love horses when I was a boy. Oh. What happened to its feet?

Vandalism, my sister said.

Is it blood? he said.

Paint, I said.

Oh. Terrible, he said. Scandalous way to treat people. Imagine them doing it now to animals too. Animals who don't know what they're on about with all their paint palaver.

He went to get us some cloths.

The horse drank half the bucket of water and we used the other half to wash down his legs and his hooves. When we dried them off they were only faintly pink.

When's the first train? I asked the man.

Now, you can't take a horse on a train, he said. Dogs is fine. But a horse.

We don't want to take him on a train, my sister said.

I asked him to tell us when the trains on this line stopped running at night and when they started again in the morning. We thanked him. He patted the horse's nose.

So soft! yet so close to the bone! he said.

He leaned down and helped dry the longer hair above one of the hooves.

Did you know that these are called the feathers? he said. It's true. Horses have feathers.

Then we took the horse through to the back of the station.

We stood and looked up and down the quiet tracks.

That direction's the way we came when we came with Leif, I said.

Years ago, my sister said.

A hundred years ago, I said.

We started walking along the stony space next to the rails.

Me and my sister, side by side and saying nothing much, heading for what we think will be home and the horse just walking with us, peaceably alongside us. Companionable, all of us following the railway track, early hours, not yet light, on the hottest of those April days before the weather broke.

What'll we do for water? He'll need it. We'll need it too.

We'll watch for rivers, streams. Anything not polluted.

How will we know it's polluted?

Scum. Dead creatures, or no creatures anywhere near it. Also, we'll watch when we pass houses for outside taps. That man at the station just gave us it when we asked. We can ask if we see the lights on in any houses, and we can ask people, when it gets too hot, to let us shelter somewhere, if they've got somewhere or if they know somewhere.

What if they say no?

If they say no we'll ask the next person, the next people. Someone will.

What'll we do for food?

Same.

We walked for four early mornings in a row. Whenever we found a good place to spend the heat of the day we stopped, once under a small stone bridge, once in a thick copse, once in a ruined structure in the middle of nowhere that had been a cafe or a restaurant with an old weatherbent sign next to it saying the words:

amilies welcome

Brave new o ld:

in my waking life since then I've been a missing person, a person missing a self, travelling a road deep underlaid with a whole other road scalding its way through to the soles of my feet every time I put one foot after the other on the surface.

My sister, not saying a word, not even the favourite *whatever*.

Here she is, back then, next to me now.

Her mouth is a firm closed line as clammed as a mystery.

Her eyes are open, lit, black and imperturbable. They look like home.

First the horse had moved with a lurch of something like delight towards what looked from the distance of the lane like a rich and perfect lawn and had thrown his head down and tried to eat it.

But it wasn't grass.

It just looked like grass.

Our house was gone. There was no house there. The front garden was gone. The back garden was gone. The houses on the street now started, as if they always had, never hadn't, at the Upshaws' house. In the space where our house and the gardens had been someone had laid an expanse of artificial grass.

I knelt down and pulled at it with my fingers. It was made of green-coloured plastic.

The horse stood about a bit on it, like we were doing now too in a daze. He wandered over past where the Upshaws had parked their cars, right where our mother's greenhouse had been, and pulled at the few still-undried tufts of grass on some of the shady places in the lane, places the weeds had grown back already even though the lane had been cleared so recently.

I was standing roughly where I'd worked out our garden gate had been. I didn't even hear the van come down the road. The first sign I had was that the horse startled and I saw it. He threw his head up and stepped backwards suddenly. Then this is what happened:

two people in riot helmets ran at me full force and knocked me over. The third picked me up off the ground by my legs and carried me upside down over to the van, put me down on the concrete. One of them put something heavy on the back of my neck, it was a foot in a boot. I heard the van doors opening. They picked me up by the collar of my T-shirt and the back band of my jeans and hurled me in so I hit myself with some force off the curved metal above a wheel. They slammed the doors.

Something was wet above my eyebrow, I'd be bleeding. The inside of the van was oven-level hot, everything metal, hot to the touch. Even so I leaned my shoulder as hard up against the back doors as I could in the hope they'd fly open as we went over the potholes like some of the doors on the campervan always used to threaten to. No luck. Out of a crack in the blackout tape on one of its back windows I watched the horse watching the van go. I shifted to the other shoulder. Behind me I could only partially see the horse, and the place our house had been, then we went round the curve and both were gone.

My sister had maybe seen the van coming before I had; she'd shouted something.

She'd surely made a run for it.

She'd be in the Upshaws' shed.

She'd have rolled herself under one of their cars and watched their feet as they passed back towards the van carrying me. She'd maybe seen my head go past upside down.

She'd have taken the shortcut at the backs of the houses into the building site. She'd be hiding in one of the hundreds of long sewage pipes or behind the brick pallets, and she'd stay there until it went dark, with any luck.

There were two men and a woman in the front seats of the van behind the metal wall; they'd taken off their helmets after they'd shut the doors on me and through the blackout crack I'd seen their faces high with heat and triumph. I'd seen their high fives. All I could see now through the crack in the blackout was blasted-back greenery then road, then people in cars who couldn't see me, then motorway, people driving along right behind me not seeing me.

I tried perching on the metal curve over the wheel but it was too hot to. The floor of the van was just as hot, the sides of it were near burning and I slid about like meat on an oily hotplate because there was nothing for me to hold on to. Nothing but this:

she'd wait until late then sneak out of the Upshaws' shed when she saw them switching their lights off and going to bed; or she'd leave it long enough for them to be asleep before she made the move. Or she'd already have rolled out from under a car and she'd get up on his back again and they'd cross through the housing estate and out into the fields and follow the river till they found somewhere cool to wait till morning. Or she'd stay hidden in the building site then come back to the street and the horse waiting, and

the van shunted to a stop. The back doors of the van got opened. I fell out.

Two people in different uniforms took me into a building by a back stair. They pushed me into a room where there were two more people, a man and a woman in medical looking clothes both with their backs to me. One asked me my name. I said nothing. They turned round. The other told me to take my clothes off and do it snappy.

I shook my head.

Oh, we've a good one here, one said.

What the fuck is it? the other said.

Can't tell, one of them said and gave me a push. The other slapped me across the head.

Which are you, then, you little weirdo? the other said.

Little moron.

One of them opened a drawer and took out a pair of longblade scissors. The other hit the back of my knees so I fell over then sat on me and pinned my legs and arms while the other cut roughly into my clothes. They stood me up again and the pieces of my clothes fell off on to the floor. They were laughing. Then they stopped laughing abruptly both at once and looked businesslike, as if laughing at me was also just another expression of the businesslike way they were dealing with me. One scanned my eyes with a handheld scanner. The other looked me over like a purchaser, checked between my fingers, behind my ears, making little disgruntled grunts as she did. Then one of them braced against me, folded me on my front on the big desk in the room and held my head pressed down on to it. The other cut most of my hair off with the scissors.

They told me what they'd decided I was.

They stood me up. One slapped me again and poked the seared place on my shoulder from the hot van door. They stood me against a white wall, filmed me standing where I was, then they filmed each of themselves laughing at, pointing at and slapping at me on the genitals.

One of them sat down.

Right. What's your name?

Name. Come on. What's your name?

Tell us a name, stupid, or we'll make up a name for you that'll get you bullied for the rest of your very short life.

Tell us it, you little cretin.

They were shouting, one at each of my ears.

Won't take long to break you.

You don't want to end up tickboxed mad, believe us you don't. Better to answer.

Better if you work with us.

I'm a –, a –, I said.

They stuttered back at me.

A – a – a –?

Little retard.

Allendale, I said.

See? Wasn't so hard. Was it.

Right. Dale. Alan. Now. Sit down, Alan, till I find you on the system.

[Pause.]

Nope, nothing. Nothing fitting this one's coming up.

Retinal?

Nothing.

Really? Nothing?

Nothing.

Weird.

If there's nothing we'll need to do it all.

[Sighs.]

Okay. Let me get the form up. Right. Date of birth place of birth ethnicity uh gender we got. Sexuality. Careful what you answer. Religion. Careful what you answer.

We're helping you here. We're going out of our way to help you. You're lucky.

Education level education level of parents job status and income level of your parents homeowner status of your parents employment or self employment of your parents postcode of your parents eh ethnicity religion gender sexuality of your parents.

They started talking among themselves about how rare it was to find one with no data trail, like landing a salmon in the days before fish ate PCBs.

What kind of a little schemer are you?

Child of a schemer family?

Good test case though. Got the looks. Worth money.

You know what that means, you? [thumping my shoulder] You should.

Take our word for it. For you it'll mean the difference between ash or diamond.

Well, diamond's maybe putting it a little strongly. But ash. Ash isn't putting it strongly. You'll be ashes. Pile of bone-ash and no one'll know.

Or give a fuck.

Well, quite a few'll have given him a fuck by then.

[Laughter.]

Don't you get it? What we're telling you. You can make this work for us *and* for you.

Error of your ways.

Made an example.

He's very photogenic. You're very photogenic, Alan.

Well, you was, till she cut your hair.

[Laughter.]

Outside the weather had broken and a storm was breaking, crazed thunder, then crazed heavy rain hitting the roof of wherever it was I was.

In my head through all of it a wide open landscape and a horse crossing it through the rain, faster than the rain, leaving the rain behind fast like speeded-up film footage from wars in history and my sister so steadfast on that horse's back that they'd melded into one single form moving at the kind of gallop that horses, horses in legends I mean, the ones that are immortal, can move at, faster than rain and wind, faster than horses in a dream, than sound, than lightning, and light, fast as all the uncatchable famous fictional horses, the one with eight legs, the one with twelve legs, the one whose tail catches on fire he's going so fast and the one so swift and gifted that he was named after lightning and the gods used him to carry thunder

and every time he hit the too-dry earth with a hoof
a pure water spring would appear under that
hoofprint, I mean the one called Pegasus, the horse
whose name became synonymous with mass
spyware, the legendary one, with the wings.

lines

rave new o ld:

processing and re-ed made me who I am today. In just five years it's taken me places I'd never have imagined possible:

the Delivery Level building where the lights never go out;

the Packing Belt. It's an apparatus that almost never stops;

the door to the office currently assigned to me;

behind it the desk, above it the cameras, there and there, on it the screens, then the chairs, and me sitting in my chair opposite the one the people sit in who are sent to my office to be checked and reported on by me. Day Shift Superior, Pickled / Preserved Goods Delivery Level Area 135. I'm in charge, I'm in charge all day like an ever ready battery.

There's the picture on the wall behind me. Superiors don't get to choose the pictures that get put on the walls in their offices. Mine says at the bottom of it that it's a photograph of a mountain range. When I catch sight of it as I come in the door it puts me in mind of the lower jaw of the open mouth of a shark.

Outside the office door, the corridor;

the other offices of the other superiors;

the lift that only superiors get to use;

the stairs that all the other staff and workers have to use;

and down below on the cellar floor of the building:

the voids.

It's a given that a void is never monitored. On any official building blueprint the voids look like stairwells, or nothing, so nobody knows they exist unless they're in the know, and the reason they do exist is that the people who use them need to avoid a record of anything that happens in them, usually to do with money or violence or sex, or all three.

The voids are where you learn what power does and what the word void can mean.

The void is simultaneously the place where, for me, words first ceased to mean and where, for words, I first ceased to mean too.

Over the past few years, most often at the start

when I was still apparently fresh enough, I was repeatedly brought to various voids by men and women more powerful than me.

That's as much of that story as I care to tell.

One line about it is more than enough.

rave ne o ld:

the first time I saw a battery injury it was on a girl a year or two younger than me.

She was placed next to me on a shuttle bus. She was sitting holding her arms away from herself strangely. I saw that she had two very bad hand burns, a bandage that suggested most of one hand was gone, the other one with a wound still weeping openly round the wrist.

She asked me to help her.

She asked me outright, out loud, performatively, like she knew they were listening.

Most likely someone had told her what to say. I was pretty sure it was a test. She started speaking more and more and soon she was speaking a torrent:

when I came into the big room the first day there

was pictures of clowns on the walls and there was a sandpit so I thought maybe it'd be play hours here as well as work hours we do all sorts of batteries there because coin batteries are also types of battery they want the manganese in them we take them apart and scrape it out there are old phone ones and zinc ones the even younger ones have to do zinc because zinc needs you to use a knife and the younger ones are more trusted with a knife because they're too stupefied to use it on anyone or themselves but I was put on the lithium ones a box of them on the table a lady showed me how to get the lithium sheets out but she had longnose pliers to do it not just her hands you go to the core she said and the lithium peels away it's easy she said you just have to remember the black strip isn't the lithium you throw it to one side then you unpeel the silver one take the plastic off it and you run really really fast with it as fast as possible to Airtight you'll be in trouble if you don't go fast with it and it changes colour well I'd opened it and got the plastic insides out I was peeling back the steel with the paperclip and it heated up in my hand I didn't know it would do that nobody told me and then there was the flare so bright so you can't even see and you can't put it out with water it eats water the boy next to me shouting get it in the sand go to the sandpit someone else one of the older ones with her hand over her eyes pushed me over there shouting stick your arms in the sand she was throwing the sand over me at least someone helped me then but now it's so sore it's way way sorer now than it was then you will won't you help me?

What I did instead was do what someone like me was supposed to do, what the farm boy's big brother had done to my sister. I said much the same kind of thing to this girl as he'd said to her.

I suppose I was lucky enough to know what was expected of me.

But the little girl looked at me. She looked baffled.

Was it maybe *not* a test, then?

She glanced at me one more time. Then she turned and looked the other way and didn't speak again.

It was quite a day. We were on our way to the Delivery Level photo session, my medal was bright on my chest. They met me off the bus, the bus drove away with the little girl on it, I ignored her when I went, she ignored me going, I can see her head in that turned-away way right now in my own head,

and they took me into the basement of the Delivery Level building where I saw for the first time the cobra coil of the Packing Belt.

rave n o :

that day was the only time I ever saw the Packing Belt not in motion.

There was a raked platform next to it, and spotlights. Then the VIPs and governors in creased and pressed and shabby and smart and perfumed and sweat smelling suits wandered through the room holding their wineglasses and were filmed raising the wineglasses and congratulating each other on the success of the Packing Belt and making the speeches.

I was standing to the side waiting.

A woman in a suit standing just in front of me was talking to a man in a suit. They were discussing how too many people had begun just overstepping, that the lines had served their purpose in their time but were now obsolete methodology.

Because fence collect transfer is the new cooking-with-gas, the man said.

Fence collect transfer. Repurpose doze resell, the woman said.

Effective example-setting plus judicious cherry-picking, the man said.

Yes. The initiative holding its own, the woman said.

Then she sensed me standing behind them. They both did; they turned. They looked vicious. I showed them my medal and I watched their faces re-form from vicious to bland to something like carrion bird.

Many congratulations, son, the man said.

They introduced me to some of the other important people. I was filmed being congratulated. One of them told me they very much approved of putting much younger fresher people like me in charge of much older people.

Then the people in suits dribbed and drabbed out of the room. The building started to judder. The Belt was starting up. Moments later the Belt was lined with people mostly Oona's age, a few younger with visible injuries, all taking things off it and packing them for delivery, taking things off it and packing them for delivery, taking things off it and packing them for delivery, taking things off it and packing them for delivery, taking things off it and packing them for delivery, taking things off it and packing them for delivery, taking things off it and packing them for delivery, taking things off it and packing them for delivery.

To teach me how to be in charge, a superior took me into a seminar room in the adjacent readjustment building for a shrink course.

These were the days when I found out what power can do.

It thickens like muscles. It's red-blooded and it tastes like blood.

The turn-away. The threatening look. The actual threat. The stony silence. The artistry and the discipline it takes to humiliate. The laughing at someone, to their face then behind their back as they walk away. The swelling pleasure of seeing someone know to shrink away from you.

The girl on that bus, for instance, the first whose head I'd made turn away.

Ghost of a sister.

There's this dream I sometimes have where my sister and I are walking down a country lane.

In the dream we're both the ages we were before our road divided.

There's a hedgerow on one side like the one on the way to where we all once lived, except the one in the dream is not ploughed up. It's all sounds of summer insects from before the summers got fucked and the birds thinned out. The verge is wildflowers, simple flowers, the kinds old poems are about; birds like I haven't heard for years except in recordings singing high in the sky or in the trees and all round us the air in the dream is the sweet smelling head-sway of grasses growing at the foot of and up the sides of a long high old stone wall the length of which my sister and I are now walking.

We arrive at a door set into this wall.

The door is a weathered old piece of planked wood with an arched top. It's thick and rain-warped, age-warped, but very tightly shut. It has no handle on its outside. There's a keyhole in the wood; the keyhole is cobwebbed and the door looks like it's maybe not been opened for years, though we can see from the place where the hinged side of it meets the wall that someone's definitely cleared the stony stuff from the foot of it and freed it up from the moss down the side of it, the marks of the removal of which are still on it like tiny scraped-in hieroglyphs.

It's me who steps forward and knocks on this door.

But it's my sister who, when the door opens inwards, goes through it.

I'm starting to go through too when a smell of singed earth hits me and it's so unlike the air on this side of the wall and so sudden and I'm so surprised by it that I reel back.

The door shuts again with her on the inside and me on the outside.

Unless this is the inside and the other side of it is the outside?

I realize I don't know the answer to that.

I knock on the door hard. It doesn't open.

I knock again. But this time my hand makes no sound. Now it's like I'm knocking on nothing but thick cloth.

I look at the wall.

Can I climb it?

Something in me says I'm not permitted to.

I call to her. I tell her I'll wait for her here.

No answer.

I sit down next to the door and lean my back against the wall. Out here, in here, is the sweet smell of grass and the yellow road stretching away back and ahead and the flowers, I can see, are starting to close their petals up, the day thinning to evening.

The dream ends with me sitting there growing more and more chilly, the cold of the wall against my lower back.

Every time I wake up with that cold at my core – even though what I've seen of her is her disappearing – I'm full of wild happiness at having seen her and walked a road with her again.

I surface each time out of this dream into relief. But relief at what?

That something in me didn't go through that door too?

Or that something in me is still there, even if just in a dream, still sitting by it? The knowledge that I'm still doing what I said I'd do, I'm waiting, I'm keeping my word?

Yes.

That at least in my dreams I still have a word I can keep.

rave n o (us):

but why can’t you just climb that wall and go too? the person called Ayesha Falcon is saying.

We are meeting in the void because the voids are never monitored. From this particular void, although it’s right at the other end of the building, you can still hear and feel the deep churn of the Belt. You can physically feel it thrum. The night shift is working now. The night shift has the worst time. We tend to assign the most damaged people the night shift.

The night shift isn’t my responsibility.

Bloody horrible in here, she says and shivers.

Yes, I say.

I sit down. She looks at the plaster dust floor.

Do I have to sit in this dust too?

You’re not obliged to do anything, I say.

So why am I here? she says.

Information, I say.

Hmm, she says.

Off the record. I want you to tell me about the cave you mentioned this morning. Where you claim that you and some others were *holed up* some years ago.

Claim? she says. You think I wasn't there?

I'm risking a lot talking to you, I say.

Think I'm risking a bit more, she says.

She shakes her head at the plaster dust everywhere. Then I see it's hard for her to sit down because of her missing hand. But she does it.

I don't offer to help.

I feel bad.

Feeling bad feels quite strange. I realize this is the first time I've felt bad, or maybe anything, for a while.

I'm sorry there's no chair in here, I say.

I'll manage, she says.

She settles herself.

This room, I say, reminds me of a room I lived in when I was a kid, by myself, in an empty house, for about a week.

And? she says.

It's a place I occasionally dream about. So. Let's treat this conversation as dream.

Nothing anyone can be held accountable for, she says.

There's this other recurring dream I have, I say. I have it quite often, and I'm thinking about it now because of something else you said to me this morning.

Which thing? she says.

I don't tell her the extended version of that dream.

I also don't tell her how, since this morning when she was put on report and I saw her see me, the memory of something I thought had been permanently deleted from me has been steadily unfurling in a snag of bright green jagged stems so that I am right now having to set my whole self hard against anything bleeding in or out of me.

I tell her instead that in the recurring dream I'm walking along next to someone who looks uncannily like me till we both arrive at a door in a wall.

We knock on it, I say. They go in first. The door shuts on me and I can't go through it. So I sit down and wait. And that's always the end of the dream.

But why can't you just climb that wall? she says. And go too? What's to stop you? It's your dream.

In the dream it's perfectly clear to me that I don't get to, I say.

Yeah but what tells you that? she says.

I shrug.

Well fuck that then, she says.

There's nothing anyone can do about what happens in a dream, I say.

If that were my dream, she says. I'd get myself ready for the next time I have it. I'd instruct myself: next time I see that wall in the dream I will make a note of each foothold, I will see exactly where to put each foot. And each hand. And then I'll be over that wall too and I'll run after them and catch up with them.

Then she laughs.

I still have both my hands, she says. In my dreams, I mean.

She looks at me, candid.

I take a sheet of the painkillers I gave her one of this morning out of my briefcase and put it on the floor between us. She eyes it. She can't not.

You want me to tell you how I lost my hand? she says. That's my big story. Well, big to me, anyway.

Tell me some more about the cave you mentioned this morning, I say.

Oh, so you *don't* want to know about me? she says laughingly.

Tell me what I'm asking first, I say.

Her eyes still on the sheet of drugs catching the light under the open bulb, she says,

okay. Well. You know. It was just some cave. A cave at the back of a rockface. It's somewhere north of here. It was in a place that used to be a tourist place, it once had a museum attached to these drawings on its walls. They were meant to be drawings of wild things, wildlife things, a cow, a deer. A bird, I remember a bird. That's why there was a museum there at all, because someone had found these lines on the walls and got excited and turned it into a place to visit.

An ibis, I say.

What's an ibis? she says.

Bird with a long beak, I say.

I don't really remember. I was mostly out of it, she says. I was lucky to get there at all. I'd been put on some official ark bus or other, I was getting taken for a checkup at the clinic because my hand wasn't healing, and when I got there someone kindly left me alone in a room with an open window. Yes. Like in a good dream.

So I rolled myself through it head first, out of there, and got myself into the town, I ducked into a hypermarket and the first thing I'd seen in there was an apple. I'd no money, I just lifted it with my good hand, ripped the plastic off it with my teeth, started eating it in the aisle, so long since I'd seen an actual apple I thought I was dreaming it too. The hypermarket people collared me and handed me over to security.

But security turned out to be the Campion, dressed up as security. I realized something else was up when we were walking along the road and they weren't stopping me eating the apple. The opposite. They were letting me eat it.

They were good people, good to me and they

didn't know me from Adam or Eve. They got me bright again and on my feet, then they took me and these other two runaways they'd picked up, they dressed us as rich tourists, they dosed us, they said no one would spot us because we were so dosed now that nobody who stopped us would believe we weren't rich people's kids.

There was an old walkway in the cave where people were once meant to be able to get quite close to the walls to see the drawings, and at the back of this there was an entrance into another space a bit like this place we're in now.

So we get through the first cave into this other cave, dark as night, darker, and then we're having to go through a crawl tunnel to another cave. I was still pretty damaged. But I did it. I had to because there was someone else coming right behind me.

The new space we come into has this hole in its ceiling that reaches the outside world so it gets a bit of actual light in there. They'd sometimes light a fire in there too, which was good because it was fucking arctic, and the damp. So the three of us get in there and there are these four other people already living there. A couple of them are in a much worse way than me, one with a lithium gouge out of her thigh, and a kid with a burn up into his face, his nose all black like he's blackened it specially like fancy-dress for a party he's decided to go to as a cat or a dog. We find out next day everybody calls him

Lassie, and he likes it, has this special barky noise he makes when you say his name, a very sweet kid, I think about him a lot, often wonder where he is now, what became of him.

The people there patchay us. They feed us.

Kindness. Bliss.

We get some sleep and when I wake up I'm maybe stuck in a cave from the beginning of history but there's an opening and I can see sky, and I'm still free.

That first night though we're sitting there pretty fucked and weirded, like we're in a tomb it's so dark.

One of the people who've been living in there starts to speak. We can't see her but we can hear her voice. She says she's going to tell us this story. She says it's called The Tyrant and the Ash.

If I could explain to you what it did for us just then to hear something so complete, a whole story, one with a beginning and an end.

I can't tell it anything like as well as she did but I'll do my best.

A tyrant runs a country. *He does this via a lot of other people doing this tyrant's work for him. They do it partly because they think he'll kill them or their families if they don't, and partly because it makes them feel powerful too.*

One of the things you're not allowed to say in this country is that the tyrant is a tyrant.

Anyway the tyrant wakes up one morning to find there's this person out there who is going round telling the populace the tyrant's a tyrant and encouraging them to say so out loud to each other.

So the tyrant has the person followed, then attacked, then beaten up and stripped of all their money. Then he has the person arrested, put in prison and occasionally tortured, and starved, and kept alone in the cold.

But the person doesn't seem broken by any of it.

The person still seems light as anything, and when anybody catches a glimpse of the person, like a guard, or another prisoner, amazingly the person is warm, witty, even funny, while still pointing out, in all their warmth and lightness and funniness, that the tyrant is a tyrant.

So the tyrant has the person killed.

He tells everyone in the country that the person who was his opponent has died of natural causes though everybody knows the person has been killed. He forbids people to see the body or to mourn the dead opponent publicly and when the person's funeral takes place he forbids people to go to the funeral, then after the funeral he has the body dug up secretly, and secretly he has it burnt. Secretly he keeps the ash that used to be the person who opposed him in a sealed container, and he keeps the container in a safe inside a larger safe in a vault inside another vault in a cellar purpose-built deep in the ground in one of his big houses.

One night when he's in that big house the tyrant can't sleep because he keeps hearing this little trembling noise, like if you could hear the sand fall inside an eggtimer, or like mortar crumbling just a little, very tiny deposits of stone coming loose every few minutes inside one of the walls of his bedroom.

Then the tyrant starts to hear this noise all round the house too.

So he goes to stay at another one of his big houses.

He has lots of big houses.

But wherever he is, whichever house he stays in, whichever of their rooms he's in, he can still hear the noise.

So he goes to spend a week on his giant yacht.

His giant yacht is even more luxurious than his houses and as big as a floating street.

He lies down on the bed in the master bedroom and closes his eyes. But there it is, even miles out at sea, the sound of stone slowly and steadily turning to powder.

Wherever he is he hears something crumbling.

It's all he can hear. It's all he can think about.

He wakes again one night and he sits upright in his bed. He knows.

It's the ash of the opponent.

It's the ash in that container that is making everything tremble.

So the tyrant goes back to his big house and has the cellar opened, and the vaults opened, and the safes opened.

He takes the container and he comes up out of the vaults into the rest of the house, into one of his luxurious bathrooms. He locks the door. He unseals and unscrews the lid of the container. He empties all that's in it into his gold toilet. He stands there in his bathroom making as sure as he can that he's got it all out of there, he even puts a finger under a tap to wet it and runs it round the insides of the container. He holds the finger well away from himself, one-handedly drops his trousers, urinates on the ash in there, then he flushes the toilet, then flushes it again.

He washes and brushes his hands and his nails very hard till his hands are raw wrist to nailtips.

He goes out to the little dock at the back of his house, fills the container that used to hold the ash with stones from his beach and throws it as far as he can into the sea.

That's done it. That's it done with. That's better.

He goes back inside, back to bed.

An hour later he wakes up in a sweat.

Is there maybe still some residue of the ash there under his fingernails?

He goes through to a different beautiful bathroom and scrubs himself all over with a brush.

Then he goes back to bed.

The next morning the first thing he does is he sends several divers out in scuba suits to find that container in the water. He tells them if they don't find it he'll send them and their partners and parents to the arks and their children to the circuses. He instructs the scientists in charge of his space programme to prepare something imminently to send a piece of debris as far from the planet as they can.

It takes a few families sent off to a few centres, but in the end one of the scuba divers comes to the surface with it.

The scientists strap it, stones and all, inside a rocket and send the rocket into outer space.

But now the tyrant is worrying that when he was shaking the rubble of the person out of the container into the toilet bowl he ingested some of the ash.

That would mean some of the person who was his opponent is now inside him.

He goes out for a walk with his dogs and his bodyguards. He worries that the ash might be in the air he's breathing.

A maid pours him a glass of water at lunchtime. He worries about the ash in the water system.

Now he doesn't want to eat.

He can't eat anything.

He's scared to drink.

He finds it hard to breathe.

He closes his eyes to the sky.

His opponent is the sky.

His opponent isn't just inside the walls of whatever room he's in.

His opponent is the walls.

His opponent is lapping at the side of his boat, at the side of his dock.

His opponent is the water.

His opponent is the air.

His opponent isn't just this world.

His opponent is the universe.

Then the voice we can hear in the dark pauses and we remember ourselves.

One of us, one of the others in the cave, says,

but does that mean he'll now try to destroy it all? The water, the air, the universe?

She's sitting in the dark, we can't really even see her and it's like the cave itself is speaking. We don't get to see what she looks like till light comes up next day, I mean the shock of how young, how thin, how not much older than we are ourselves.

And the shock for me, this morning, of how much she looked like you. Because when I saw you it was like seeing her through a mist.

And this is what she tells us, back then in the dark place, as an end to this story, her voice in that dark, saying,

maybe he'll try. Why not? He's mad. He's a tyrant. He thinks he's all-powerful.

But look at what real power is.

The person he turned into a mound of nothing but rubble, nothing but smoke and ash, is the opposite of destroyed.

His opponent is everywhere.

His opponent is everything.

ave n (i) r :

sublime, I say.

I say it out loud.

Yes, she was, the person called Ayesha Falcon says. Sublime.

Only I have the right to think my sister was sublime, I think to myself,

but I don't say.

Pretty sure the Campion brought us there first so we could get what they called intact again, the person is saying.

She holds up her arm with no hand.

Which you'd think impossible, right? The impossible possible. Well. That's what she was.

What she was.

Only I have the right, if anyone ever has, to consign my sister to a past tense, but I don't say.

Unbelievable believable hope. She told us the story of the mother, the person called Ayesha Falcon says, a mother so outraged by what's happened to her child that this mother makes the mountains pick themselves up and move. And the story of the person who was really a swan and the swan who was really a person. And the traveller who, wherever they go, is accompanied by a flower that never dies.

She pauses.

I told you already, I say. I don't have a sister. I never had a sister.

Yeah, you never had the sister who you look so like that I thought when I saw you you *were* her. The one who told us she learned everything from you.

Kind of thing people imagine a sister would say, I say.

She shakes her head at me, impatient.

Your sister told us that because of you anyone could be anything and everything. And I mean. Look at you now. Living the best life, eh? Rose through the ranks –

she sees me flinch and we both know she meant me to flinch –

got yourself verified against the odds, oh, so well done, big congratulations on your multiple state promotions. Not just verified. Awarded all the way to Delivery Level superior. Re-education Man of the Moment. God. I remember those ceremonies well. We had to sit through so fucking many of them.

She looks at me with wild eyes. For a moment I don't know what she'll do and I'm actually scared because there's no button to press in this non-room to alert any security.

But all she does is, she scrapes up some of the plaster dust and rubble off the floor in the hand she still has and then she throws it at me. It doesn't reach me, she's on the other side of the room and it's just dust. But I can see its filaments falling in the air, and I sneeze, and she laughs.

I laugh too.

The sneeze of truth, she says.

Then she says,

bless you.

I wipe at my nose.

Unbelievable believable hope, I say. Impossible, possible.

Then I am momentarily businesslike again. I sit forward. She sees this and a worried look crosses her face and I remember for the splinter of a moment the businesslike faces of the people who processed me.

But fuck that, and them, because my briar self is back, prickly and twined and opening in me like a bush covered in wild opening blossom.

Have you any more information for me? I say.

She leans her head back against the wall, closes her eyes, opens them, looks at me.

Well, she says. If I were ever to give you, which I never will, the *information* about how they bulldozed our house, and went on to do the same to the houses of every family in our street and all the other people in our town who happened to be designated what they'd decided was unacceptable.

She holds up her ruined wrist, the one that ends in no hand, smiles a gentle smile at me and says with equal gentleness,

I'd tell you so you couldn't not feel this gone hand in yours.

Brave old world:

one day our mother, who had been so miserable that for weeks we hadn't been out much or done much of anything, had suddenly jumped up, gathered us up and belted us both into the campervan.

She drove us playing the songs by the singer called Marianne Faithfull up the lane and on to the main road then up the motorway towards the greener north. Broken English, Sister Morphine, Working Class Hero, What Have They Done To The Rain.

You are sister morphine, I said to my sister. Who are you? Say it. Sister morphine.

Leave your sister, our mother called back from the front.

My sister was examining a hair caught in her

fingers. She kicked at the back of the seat in front of her. At this point she was still saying nothing, four years old and wordless. She'll talk when she's ready, our mother said to anyone who questioned it.

We parked the campervan in the car park and walked to what our mother called the gorge. It was green, very long, pocked with a dozen different caves. The guide who took us on the tour had a namebadge on. *Nicole*. She told us how to see what shapes the lines people had carved in the walls of one of the caves might be making and said it was called cave art.

One piece of cave art looked like a giant walking tusk. The guide said it was a bird, or a woman, or maybe both. She showed us what she said was a stag. At first I couldn't see it. It looked like rockface. Then it suddenly turned into a stag! Then I moved my head and it disappeared again, like it could appear and disappear at will.

In one place the carved lines and the curve of the wall really clearly resembled a bird's beak and neck. The guide said it was an ibis.

Birds, bears and wolves, bison and wild dogs, wild horses; they'd all lived here and used these caves as somewhere to shelter, and so did the people who lived here, in fact people cooked and ate creatures in this cave we were standing in and creatures ate and got eaten by other creatures here too, she said.

The guide wrote the words ibis and palaeolithic down for me on a Starbucks receipt she had in her pocket.

Have you ever considered that the word engrave also has the word grave in it? she said leaning on my mother's back as she wrote them. And how very close the people who made these marks on the walls are to us when you see their drawings, even though they've been nothing but bones and dust now for all those thousands of years?

Our mother gave her some money to say thank you for the tour. Then we went to a place full of glass cases. The people who'd lived in these caves had converted the bones of things into the needles and other useful tools on display in these cases. There were stones too, which they'd made into axes or knives to kill and skin some of the animals that lived here so they could eat them and wear them.

Our mother lifted my sister up so we could all look into one glass case at the same time. In it was a piece of bone the length of the palm of our mother's hand.

It was a rib bone, the information card said, but it didn't say whose or what's. It was apparently relatively recent, only twelve thousand years old. Someone had carved the head of a horse on to it, with its short mane shocking forward on its neck, and its collarbone, its jaw, its mouth, its nostril, its single open eye. There were lines scratched vertically across the horse like the horse was behind a fence. There were also a lot of horizontal lines scratched along the length of it which made the horse look like it was animated, moving at speed.

These horizontal and vertical lines, the information card said, had been added to the horse much later, maybe to try to ruin or erase the picture.

I looked at it and wondered how it was possible that somebody could have been angry at – or anything other than impressed by – lines scraped on a bone that looked so very like a horse.

The information card said it was the oldest piece of portable art ever found in this country. Our mother, who was holding my sister's arm away from the glass case which she was trying to hit with her hand, told us this meant someone could pick up this bone that was also a picture and put it in a pocket and take it with them when they travelled. Which you couldn't really do with that ibis on the wall, could you?

A god could, I said.

Well, yes. Nobody and nothing else would have a big enough pocket, our mother said. Or a big enough front room to hang it in.

On the way back home in the campervan I looked at the words on the receipt that the guide had given me.

Java Frappuccino.

Mini Ciabatta.

Palaeolithic.

Ibis.

But did you both enjoy yourselves today? our mother called to us in the back.

Yes, thank you, I said.

What about you, Rose? our mother said.

Horse, my sister said.

My mother turned so astonished in her seat that the campervan swerved a little. She turned quick back round again to face forward shouting at the road coming towards us,

what did she say? Did she just speak?

My sister spoke again. This time she sounded indignant.

I said *horse*, she said.

Brave you world:

I've got to get home, I say in the void.

Lucky you, the person called Ayesha Falcon says. Something called a home to go to.

You're in the hostel system?

She nods.

I know the system. It's a filthy system, narrow, dark, flea-bitten, bedbug rife, no privacy, five of you to a room if you're lucky and you have to sign in and out with a *security guard* who's there *for your own good* every time you leave or come back.

She gets herself to her feet. I see she's having trouble doing it. I don't offer to help. I stand and dust the plaster off my clothes. She tries to do the same.

Then I actually do it. I reach my own arm forward and help dust her down.

She looks at me, amazed.

Before we leave the void I give Ayesha Falcon the sheet of double painkiller. Then I think again. I take the whole packet, sixty sheets, out of my briefcase. I offer it to her. She looks at me like she can't believe her eyes.

Really?

If they're of use, I say.

I can barter these, she says.

I tell her to be sure to get herself off them as soon as she's able because Patchay's more than laced with what people used to call heroin. I tell her the name of a good doctor who'll help with this and tell her to tell this doctor that I sent her.

Then I hand her my apartment key.

What? she says.

I tell her the address of my apartment.

Leave it for a bit, just a couple of weeks, then it's yours. If they ask you, you don't know anything about me, and you won the apartment in a wager. Lower your expectations, it's not much of a space but there's a bed, and it's comfortable enough there, and private, nobody else, I won't be there. Think of it as yours.

She looks at the key in her hand then looks at me.

Where will you be?

Elsewhere.

You going rogue? she says.

She shakes her head.

Don't. They'll trace you, she says.

Maybe, I say. Maybe not.

They'll ark you, she says.

If they do, at least it'll be me it happens to, I say. And one last question, if I may.

You're the boss, she says.

Where is she? I say.

She laughs.

You're not the boss of that, she says.

I nod.

Okay, I say. Thank you.

I turn towards the door with one arm slightly extended away from myself because that's what you do when a meeting's over. She sees this and naturally turns towards the door too, as if dismissed. The automata of authority.

I hold my hand out as if to shake her hand. She holds her two arms out in front of her.

Which hand would you like? she says.

Both, I say.

Brave now world:

I walk back through the building and I unlock my office.

Strange. I notice I'm now not worried about anything.

The first thing I do is disable the room cameras. I do this by climbing up on the desk and draping them with my coat, my jacket and my hat and by pressing keyboard-override on sound. I block the camera holes on my screen, the obvious one and the hidden one, with folded pieces of blank paper from the printer drawer. Then I speakerphone Ben in security in case he looks at the screenbank and sees my screens are blanking. I tell him my cameras aren't working properly and ask him to make a note of it for tomorrow's rota.

Right-o, Mr Allendale, he says.

That's not my name, I say. I'm not Mr anything.

Right-o, Mr Allendale, Ben says.

I disconnect. I sit down at my desk.

I bring up all the information there is on Ayesha Falcon and scrub her work history, exchange her work registration from Packing Belt to Organic Nadorcott, backdate it so she'll get backdated pay and head-office ratify it. The Organic Nadorcott sector is as good as it gets. There's demand for organic nadorcotts among the people who have the money to afford organic nadorcotts, which have to be grown with care and cultivated with patience. This makes for a much less harried workforce. The pay is better, the hours are laxer, the food is healthier, the accommodation is communal and high end, the team is friendly.

I also know it's a good solid Campion recruitment place.

I get up. I stretch my arms and legs.

I go round my own desk and sit in the seat where all the people who've been sent to my office have sat to be reported on. I've never sat in it before.

Here I'm facing my own empty chair. I can't not be overwhelmed by the size of the picture of the mountain range, dark its sea of snow-capped eye teeth that seems to go on forever, then the fury of the red sky of its sunset above and how it must have looked to everyone who sat in that chair like it was rising over me big as a smashed-in jaw.

Old shrink trick. Be in awe.

I shake my head. I'm laughing like I'm a child.

It is this simple.

I stand up, go back behind my desk again. I get the list up on screen of our current complete Packing Belt workforce. I switch every name on the Packing Belt list, from the lowliest Belt worker all the way to the top engineer, to Organic Nadorcott. I head-office ratify it and initiate Messager so everyone knows they've been re-registered and will with immediacy right now already have a copy of their employment ratification certificate.

This will scupper Delivery Level for roughly three days.

To scupper it even further I access the supercomputer hard drive and delete at source all the Delivery Level technical data.

Now nobody here will know how to keep the apparatus going.

After that I delete as much ARC and CRC data as I have access to.

Finally I delete all my own data.

I watch the facial maps disappear from three systems and then I clear, scrub and disinfect the systems of me.

There.

Now that I don't exist I finally exist again.

I try taking a deep breath.

Packing Belt air.

It won't take them long to be on to me. Three days? I hope it's long enough.

Amazing to be thinking those words together again: *hope*, and *I*.

I unlock the drawer and take out a pencil. I take a metal sharpener. I put them in my pocket. I go to lock the drawer again, then I don't, I leave it hanging open. They'll think I've been robbed and kidnapped. Heh! I'm the thief of me, leaving the office and walking through the building, waving to the security hut, holding up the sharpener so Ben can see it in case it sets off the scanner, and Ben opens the gate for me without asking to see my pass. Lucky; my pass won't work now. My car pass won't work either. I don't care. I leave the car in the car park. I walk past and don't look round till I'm out of the complex.

When I can't feel the building thrumming behind me any more I loosen my collar. More, I stop and unbutton all the buttons. I rip the whole collar off my work shirt.

That's better.

I slide the work belt out of my work trousers and coil it up and leave it neatly on a wall.

When I get to where the river leaves the city behind I stop on the big bridge, strip myself of all devices and leave everything that's supposed to say who and what I am on the pavement in a tidy pile, very like someone who's jumped.

I can't jettison my retinas, or my fingerprints.

But I can use them, for a while at least, for as long as I get away with it, as if retinas and fingerprints are something to do with what eyes do and what hands do.

Where have I been?

Wherever it was, I'm back.

What was it she once said?

I am all my me's.

An alert will have gone out by now about an unverifiable standing dangerously close to the edge of the bridge. The cameras above will be signalling possible suicide. It's commonplace. A lot of unverifiables jump. Their bones are down in the rock and the sand of the riverbed.

I turn and wave and smile at the one camera I can see. They'll think a deranged person is waving at them. They won't care. Nobody bothers to record the people who jump off the bridge any more. The red tape that comes with it is too much work.

Colon! I shout at the camera up on top of the bridge.

Campervan!

This bridge has no sound surveillance. When the people in intelligence eventually work out it's me they will spend ages trying to decipher this and they will never in a million years have any idea what it is I'm really saying.

I'm laughing right now, soundlessly, on screens somewhere.

I also know exactly where the camera blind spots are.

The CC system is shonky on purpose, to let people be disappeared.

Bravo new world:

I'm obsolete, romantic.

It's a start.

I will put one foot after another.

I'll get to the edge of what's built up, where the new meets the old industrial. That landscape is poisonous and I've no mask. Never mind, tie my handkerchief over my mouth and nose like a bandit and leave the road behind where the road leaves the river behind, follow the river north as close to the riverbank as possible.

The river, I can see even from up here on the bridge, is filthy. The water warnings are still pinned up everywhere. But it's a river. That means source. As I get further towards it maybe the river will start looking less wan. There'll maybe still be birds there. There'll be trees.

If I don't find somewhere to shelter I'll let the weather have me. Whatever.

On the way to whatever, one of the things I'm bound to pass is a field that's got horses in it out in the weather too, white, brown, black, grey, all the colours of horse.

They'll be massive and delicate, strong as horses.

I know how to hold my arm out with my hand open towards them. Maybe one or two of them will see me do this, raise their heads, maybe even start to cross that field towards me.

Brave new word:

silence in the courtroom! The monkey's going to speak! Speak, monkey, speak!

You're a girl on a horse.

You are eleven years old.

You don't know why you're thinking of that old silence game now. It was a good game. Your mother played it with you both. It meant that whoever spoke next had revealed themselves to be a monkey not a person. It was one of her funniest ways of getting you to shut up when she wanted peace. It was its funniest ever, though, when one day you both became the monkey, first you spoke in pretend monkey language then Bri spoke back at you like they could speak it too and understood what you'd said and were answering, and it was as if you were both really having a conversation. All of which made your mother laugh and call you her best beloved pair of monkeys.

The round blue glass top off her perfume bottle was on top of the bags of rubbish in the neighbours' dustbin, it was nestled in some of the packaging that came with the perfume. No bottle, you looked for it but couldn't see the bottle, just the top off it, in what was left of the white cardboard container. You picked that round blue thing, a bit like a little globe, out of there. You felt for the place where the hole through it was, where the spraytop of the bottle had once fitted neatly inside it.

You put the globe to your nose.

It still had the smell of her.

How did it get into a dustbin?

You pushed it into your front pocket.

There is no way she is back, or anywhere near here.

There would have been no stopping her if she were.

No. Tell it like this:

whatever's stopping her, there will be no stopping her.

You stood in the place where your home no longer was and you stared up at the brand new upstairs window big as a double door in mid air in the side of the next door neighbours' house. That wall used to be the inside wall of your own house.

The bricks had all been painted white to look like the wall has never not been the outside wall of their house. But you could still make out the thicker brick lines under the paint. Those lines marked the places some of the rooms of the house you were all living in not very long ago once had a floor or ceiling.

The neighbours were looking down out of that new window. You could see the whole of both of them from head to foot, life size, staring down at you standing below them on the green plastic like they thought you couldn't see them.

But you were life size too.

You stood every inch of yourself and you stared straight back at them.

You bent and picked up a stone from the place the plastic grass met the earth at the edge and you held the stone, a good size stone, up in the air to show them what you had.

They flinched backwards away from their window.

When they dared themselves back to look out of it again you let them see you choosing not to throw it, let them watch you drop that stone.

You didn't take your eyes away from them though, until one of them, the man, raised a phone to his ear.

You shook your head at them then.

The slam of thunder all round you.

You picked up the stone you'd dropped again. You showed them how you were tucking it in your pocket, as if to say you'll be back with it.

You walked backwards, still with your eyes on them, across the grass that wasn't grass, and when you got to the horse you turned, put your hands on his neck and back and jumped, pulled yourself up on to him, twisted round on your front on his back, then your leg round and over, and you sat up straight.

The horse waited while you did this, patient.

Then the rain started. It came down like a heavy curtain.

Because of the rain they won't have seen where you went.

Now you're coming through the storm.

You are heading north.

You're soaked to the skin. So is the horse.

The rain stops.

You are staying off the roads, crossing the fields when there's hedge or woods for cover and no one can track you too plainly.

What will you do now?

First you'll watch for somewhere good to stop so you can try to dry this horse down a bit.

You will need something with an edge, not too sharp, to scrape the rain off.

Because you lived so near here not very long ago, and because you know a lot about what happens round here, you know you are about to go through fields that have been sprayed with stuff that the horse had best not eat.

You suggest to the horse to stop by shifting yourself on his back. He does. You slide yourself down on to the ground and walk him to the edge of the crop. You keep your hand on his neck so he knows to keep his head up as you both walk along.

You start occasionally glancing at the ground passing beneath the horse's belly and legs in case of good flat stones or pieces of wood.

You could use the side of your hand to make the rain run off him if you can't find anything better. You try it now for a moment as you walk, yes, that works a bit, the water does run off as you push against the flank. It's not the best way, but if you have to, it will do.

What about the stone you've got in your pocket?

You take it out and look at it. It has a blunt edge. It might actually do it quite well.

But behind you now there's someone shouting. The horse hears him first. You turn and look to see what the horse heard.

A boy is running across the field through the crop, whatever it is, green shoots beaten flat by the rain.

It's that boy from the farm.

Now that he's seen you see him he shouts your name, stops running, holds his sides. Then he waves.

Come on, you say to the horse.

You both start walking again, same direction you were going in.

The boy catches up with you half a field later.

Wait, he says.

No, you say.

But then you stop and turn.

Did you follow us all the way? you say. Did you see what happened to us?

You haven't, he says, stopping with his hands on his sides again, breathing hard. Paid, he says.

Then more breathing hard.

In full, he says.

Okay, you say. But I haven't any more money right now.

My father's, he says. Horse.

Fine. Here. Take him back. You take him. On you go. Jump on.

He won't let me do that, he says.

You can walk beside him then, you say. Go on. Take him.

I haven't any rope, he says.

You could use your shirt, you say. You can tie its sleeves round his neck and use that as a rope.

Oh, he says. Yes.

He takes off his shirt. He is barechested under it and it makes you feel sorry about him or for him, feel something sorry anyway, he looks so strangely pink uncovered.

He ties the two sleeves together round the horse's neck under the jaw. He pulls.

Move, he says to the horse.

The horse doesn't.

You look at the boy's feet, his wet shoes, and you can see the red paint stain that's a broad line across one of them. The boy sees you see this. You raise your eyebrows at the boy. You start walking away from him and the horse in the direction you were going in all along. The horse starts forward to follow you, you knew he would, and the boy tries to stop him, pulls on the knotted shirt, links his arms through it and uses his whole weight to try to stop the horse, and the horse, no effort at all, drags the boy along with him, the boy's feet dragging through the clay.

When you look round again the horse is coming nodding towards you with the strange noose of the shirt hanging loose round his neck. The boy is flat on his front behind him down in the clay.

You keep going.

But there the boy is, slopping behind you again, wet-clay-stained now all up his calves and his shorts and his chest, all the way up to his face, even clay in his hair.

He looks like a boy made of mud.

Where are you going? he shouts behind you.

You ignore him.

You owe us! he says.

You laugh to yourself and ignore him, keep going, the horse coming hoof after hoof beside you.

I did, he says. I did see what happened.

You stop but you don't turn. The horse stops alongside you.

I want to help, he says behind you.

You turn to look at him.

I think it's wrong, he says.

You nod.

How do we make it not wrong? he says.

We solve it, you say.

How? he says.

We solve it by salving it.

What does that even mean? he says.

You see the smear of clay down the side of his face, above his eye the clay thick across his eyebrow. You put your hands in your pockets to see if you've got anything on you that you can help clean him up with. In your back pocket there's something, you take it out, what is it? a wedge of wet folded paper. You peel it carefully open because it's stuck together and the handwriting on it has run.

The words are only bits of words, lines of blurred or smeary words with the occasional whole word.

Guff?

no, it's gliff –

gliff me hor momen esembl chance glanc right fain trace inkl evade scape glimm unanticipat light

Behind you the horse steams and stamps in all the wet and the heat and the reality very like a horse in a story. You go over and untie the knot in the shirt still hanging off his neck and you pat with the flat of your hand the place where his mane stops and his back begins. He likes you doing this. You take his long head in your hands and you speak calm at his ear.

Two minutes. Let me just sort this.

Then you go back over to the boy and you use the wet wedge of paper from your pocket to clean the clay off the side of his face and rub what you can of the clay out of his eyebrow. He looks at you when you do this with a look so open and needy that it's quite frightening. You give him back his own wet-through shirt. He pulls it on over his shoulders and clay-smeared chest and buttons it all the way up to the collar again.

You fold the muddied paper and put it back in the pocket you took it out of and you turn, start walking.

The horse starts walking.

The boy starts walking too.

We'll be making it up as we go, you tell them both over your shoulder.

Endpaper artwork: Dora Carrington, *Iris Tree on a Horse*, *c*.1920s (oil, ink, silver foil and mixed media on glass) © Ingram Collection of Modern British and Contemporary Art/Bridgeman Images